D1267693

Brumby Mountain

DIAMOND
SPIRIT

ALSO IN THE
DIAMOND SPIRIT
SERIES
BY KAREN WOOD

Diamond Spirit

Moonstone Promise

Opal Dreaming

Golden Stranger

5
DIAMOND
SPIRIT

Brumby Mountain

KAREN WOOD

ALLEN&UNWIN
SYDNEY•MELBOURNE•AUCKLAND•LONDON

First published in 2012

Copyright © Karen Wood 2012

All rights reserved. No part of this book may be reproduced or
transmitted in any form or by any means, electronic or mechanical,
including photocopying, recording or by any information storage
and retrieval system, without prior permission in writing from the
publisher. The *Australian Copyright Act 1968* (the Act) allows a
maximum of one chapter or ten per cent of this book, whichever is
the greater, to be photocopied by any educational institution for its
educational purposes provided that the educational institution
(or body that administers it) has given a remuneration notice
to Copyright Agency Limited (CAL) under the Act.

Allen & Unwin
83 Alexander Street
Crows Nest NSW 2065
Australia
Phone: (61 2) 8425 0100
Fax: (61 2) 9906 2218
Email: info@allenandunwin.com
Web: www.allenandunwin.com

Cataloguing-in-Publication details are available from the
National Library of Australia
www.trove.nla.gov.au

ISBN 978 1 74237 863 3

Cover photos by iStockphoto / Eileen Groome (girl and horse), cynoclub
(girl's face), Gary Radler (background), Björn Kindler (storm clouds)
Cover and text design by Ruth Grüner
Set in 11.3 pt Apollo MT by Ruth Grüner
This book was printed in July 2014 at McPherson's Printing Group,
76 Nelson St, Maryborough, Victoria 3465, Australia.
www.mcphersonsprinting.com.au

3 5 7 9 10 8 6 4

MIX
Paper from
responsible sources
FSC® C001695
www.fsc.org

The paper in this book is FSC® certified.
FSC® promotes environmentally responsible,
socially beneficial and economically viable
management of the world's forests.

For Anthony

1

JESS HUNCHED HER shoulders against the wind as she watched Opal prance around the paddock on knobbly long legs, nostrils flaring. Dodger followed and together they galloped through the long grass with sudden bursts of speed and frantic skidding around corners. Dodger stopped abruptly at the top of the hill and trumpeted across the valley.

'Come on, you big wild boy,' Jess called, and walked into the paddock with a steaming molasses and bran mash. It smelled so good she could have eaten it herself. 'Get it while it's hot!'

The old stockhorse gave one last snort and trotted across the slope towards her, succumbing to the temptation of the feedbin. Opal followed and ducked in under his neck to take a mouthful too.

Jess ran a hand along the filly's neck. The time out

west on Lawson's cattle station had done her good. She was a yearling now, taller at the rump than at the wither. Her woolly coat was a deep liver colour, unbroken but for three white spots over her left shoulder. One ear stood proud, the other flopped at a funny angle, something that Jess found endearing. She didn't mind if Opal wasn't perfect.

As the horses devoured the feed, Jess grabbed her saddle and bridle from the shed. Today, her boyfriend, Luke, and his stepbrother, Lawson, were coming home with a truckload of wild horses from New South Wales. Soon it would be time to ride over to Harry's place to help get the brumbies settled, and see Luke again.

Jess slung a rope around Opal's neck, then mounted Dodger and rode down the driveway with the filly trotting along behind. The horses knew the track to Harry's place well. Although Harry had died a couple of years ago, Jess and her friends still met at his stables often. Luke, as his adopted son, still lived there with Harry's widow, Annie.

When Jess arrived, Grace was perched on the yard rail, texting, in old joddies, thongs and a baggy fur-lined hoodie. 'About time!' she said, tucking her phone back into her pocket and jumping off the rail. 'I wish the truck would hurry up and get here too! I can't wait to check out the brumbies.'

'Me too,' said Jess. 'Hey, maybe one of them will be *your* dream horse, Gracie.'

'Surprise!' Shara burst out of the stable block and did a star jump, making Opal startle.

Jess gave an elated squeal. 'What are *you* doing here? You're supposed to be at boarding school!'

'Corey drove down and picked me up. He brought me home for the weekend,' said Shara. 'He knew I was busting to see the brumbies. And to see you.'

Jess slipped off Dodger and hugged her best friend.

Grace's phone jingled. 'That'll be them!' She pulled it out and read the message. 'It's from Lawson. They're on Coachwood Road. The horses'll be here any minute!' She jumped off the fence. 'Let's open the gates!'

Jess felt her heart beat faster in her chest. She could hear the truck coming, groaning and hissing around the last bend. She saw its dirty red cabin, like a bald sunburnt head, appear above the line of trees. Hooves stomped and banged in the crate behind. But it wasn't the horses that had her all wound up.

She led Dodger and Opal to the stable block, grinning at the floor. Doing something useful might stop her from dancing on the spot and making a total git of herself.

The truck gave a final hiss as the brakes released. As Jess shut Opal inside a stable, she heard a door slam. Back outside, she saw Lawson walk around the nose of the truck in his standard jeans, shirt and peaked cap. Two wolf-like dogs leapt out of the passenger side, one after the other, and then came Luke.

Jess stood back and drank him in – tall, lanky, all rumpled hair and dirty jeans. He reached back into the cabin for a tattered mustering hat and clamped it onto his head, then hauled out a rolled-up swag. He cast a glance about the property and stopped at Jess. She smiled. On the outside she was calm, but on the inside she was leaping about like a puppy itching to be let off its chain.

Within moments Luke was surrounded by excited, noisy people. Tom ran down from the house and started punching him. Annie called out from the front door and shuffled down the pathway, wiping floury hands on her apron. Grace climbed the side boards of the truck and peered in through the gaps. Grunter the pig squealed and screeched. The dogs barked.

Jess laughed. It was a mad scene. It always was when one of the gang came home.

Luke threw his swag over one shoulder and a bag over the other. 'As soon as I dump my gear you're dead meat, Tom!' He walked towards the small stable that was his living quarters at the property, catching Jess's eye again briefly before Tom pushed his hat down over his head.

The pair of them disappeared through the flat door. Jess heard laughing and wrestling. Something smashed.

She rolled her eyes and led Dodger to the end stable. 'Boys,' she said as she let herself in, giving the gelding a quick rub on the forehead.

Within minutes she heard the sound of boots coming down the stable aisle. The quiet clink of the door latch. Three steps through soft wood shavings.

'Hey.'

She spun around. 'Hey!'

He grinned and held out his arms. She leapt into them, twined herself around him and took in his hair, his skin, his warm, bristly neck. She squeeeezed him.

He lifted her up and squeezed her in return. 'Missed you,' he whispered into her hair.

She pulled back and looked at him, beaming. There was so much she wanted to ask. Where had he been? What had he done? Why had he been gone so long?

He beamed back at her, and in his eyes she could see a million thoughts buzzing in his head. His mouth opened and he inhaled, as though he was about to tell her something amazing.

'Ahem!' Lawson stood in the doorway, clearing his throat. 'You guys gonna help get these brumbies off the truck?'

'No!' they said in unison.

'Suit yourself,' Lawson muttered, and he disappeared down the stable aisle.

'Oh my God, come and look at this!' Grace yelled from somewhere outside. 'Where's Jess?'

Luke groaned. 'We should go help them.'

'No we shouldn't.'

'Yes we should.'

'No we shouldn't.'

'You're right, we shouldn't.'

Jess sighed. 'We probably should.'

'No we shouldn't.'

Jess laughed and reached for the stable door. The questions could wait. 'Coming!' she called. She looked at Luke and felt a rush of excitement. 'Let's get them unloaded!'

2

LUKE'S ENTHUSIASM DIDN'T seem to match Jess's. Something of a warning flashed across his face. Jess looked at him with surprise. 'What's wrong?'

'Those brumbies were caught by brumby-runners. Lawson didn't want to take them, they were too . . .' Luke paused, as though lost for a description, ' . . . bad.'

'What do you mean?'

At that moment, Lawson rolled the back door of the stock crate to one side and Jess saw the four horses inside. They were brumbies all right, with rolling eyes and wild, snorty nostrils. Their flanks were hollow and their hips poked out like coathangers. 'See what you mean,' she said.

'John's on his way over,' said Luke. 'I already rang him.'

Jess nodded approval. John Duggin was the local vet.

As she looked over the brumbies her pity turned to

shock. There were two mares, one bay and one creamy white, with swollen, cut legs. A buckskin foal had welts around its neck that looked like rope burns, and large patches of skin off its face.

The fourth was a palomino stallion, tall and well-built, but his tail, Jess noticed, was stripped of hair and had sores all over it. It hung crookedly to one side. 'His tail's broken.'

'Look at his *face*,' said Shara, joining her in the doorway.

The entire side of the stallion's face was one nasty wound, with pus seeping out of it. Even more startling were his eyes, like ice-blue sapphires.

Jess stared. There was something unnerving about those arctic eyes. They were strangely human, and somehow drew her deep inside the wretched creature's soul.

'Shame they ran him,' said Lawson, hopping up onto the side of the truck and looking in. 'He'd have been a good horse.'

'Ran him? What do you mean?' asked Grace.

'They chase them with horses and dogs until they're exhausted. When they catch a brumby, they tie its head and tail to the side of a truck and drive away, dragging it alongside. It's the only way they can get them out of the bush. There's no way they could get them up a ramp.'

'He must have fought really hard,' added Luke, 'for his tail to be broken like that.' He looked away.

'How could anyone *do* that?' whispered Jess.

'Makes you sick, doesn't it,' said Luke. 'Angry, too. I could—' He bit off the rest of what he was about to say. 'Step back and give them some space,' he said instead, hopping down off the rails. 'They're a bit freaked out.'

The brumbies huddled in a corner. 'They don't know what gateways are,' said Luke.

'We should draft out the stallion to start with,' said Lawson. 'He needs a vet, big time.' He leaned over the side of the trailer and tapped at the stallion with a long hollow pole. The horse pinned its ears back and lunged, smashing against the truck wall with a deafening clatter.

Lawson swore and leapt off the side of the truck.

'They're going to hurt themselves even more if we don't get them out quickly,' said Jess. 'How long have they been in there?'

'Too long,' said Lawson. He looked towards the stables. 'We need a coacher – a domestic horse to show them the way out.' His eyes came back to Jess. 'You bring that filly over today?'

'Opal?'

He nodded.

'I'm not putting her in there!'

'You don't have to,' he said. 'Just lead her to the bottom of the ramp, to show them where to go.'

'That stallion would kill her!' She glared at Lawson. 'Put your own horse in there!'

'Mine's too old. We need a young horse – one that's submissive, non-threatening.' He held her gaze. 'A filly.'

Jess shook her head and folded her arms firmly across her chest. 'Not a chance!'

'What about in the mares' paddock?' suggested Luke. 'Are any of Biyanga's foals handled?'

'Only the colts,' said Jess. 'They came up to be gelded. None of the fillies leads very well yet.'

As she spoke, one of the mares squealed and kicked out at the metal walls with a crashing blow. It stirred the whole mob up. They scrambled up the side, threatening to jump out.

'They won't hurt her, Jess,' said Luke. 'Brumbies are different to domestic horses. They have different instincts.'

Jess looked at the wild animals in the back of the truck and snorted. 'Yeah, I can see that!'

The brumbies gradually settled again and everyone seemed to go quiet. Jess looked around and noticed that everyone was staring at her, saying nothing.

'What?' she demanded.

'Nothing,' said Grace.

'Jess—' Shara broke off.

Tom looked away.

Lawson was still eyeballing her. Luke turned to her pleadingly.

She gave him a pained look. For the first twelve months of Opal's life the filly had been racked with illness and there'd been times when Jess had thought she wouldn't survive. How could Luke ask her to put Opal at risk again? 'She's been through enough. She's only just come good. If she got hurt again . . .'

'They won't hurt her.'

'They will.'

'She only needs to walk onto the ramp and come out again. She doesn't have to go all the way in there.'

'Oh my God, the bay one's fallen over,' Grace suddenly shouted. 'They're standing on her!'

'Okay, okay,' Jess jumped off the fence and raced for the stables.

'Opal,' she called softly.

Jess took the rope from the hook on the wall and walked calmly to the filly, slipping it around her neck and pulling her away. 'We need your help, girl.'

Lawson stood at the gate to the yards, holding it open for her. 'Do you want me to take her in there?'

'No,' she said, giving him an *as-if* look. He rolled his eyes.

Jess led Opal into the yards and Lawson closed the

gate behind her. The ground was muddy and churned up. The filly put her nose down and sniffed.

'Can you get her to walk up there?' asked Lawson, nodding towards the ramp.

'In a minute,' Jess said, not wanting to be rushed. She wasn't sure if Opal could even do this. She had only ever trained her at home, never in strange surroundings.

She led Opal to the truck, gave a quiet cluck and pointed up the ramp. 'Walk up.' Opal put one hoof out and placed it cautiously on the metal. It was different to the timber one at home, making a clanging noise instead of a thud. She scuttled backwards.

Jess brought her back to the ramp. 'Walk up,' she repeated. After a few more attempts, she managed to get Opal to put her front hooves on the loading ramp. The filly stretched out her neck and peered into the truck, sniffing curiously.

The creamy mare clattered across the truck with her ears pricked.

No one else made a sound. Grace and Shara were crouched behind the fence, out of the way, watching through the lower rails. The boys stood well back. Opal took another step up the ramp. Jess glanced anxiously at Lawson.

He made a quiet gesture and nodded. 'Let her go in,' he mouthed.

Jess shook her head. 'No,' she mouthed back.

He scowled.

She tugged softly on the rope, asking Opal to back out again, but the filly pulled against it and walked another few steps up the ramp. She sniffed some more. The creamy mare sniffed in return, with short, anxious puffs. Opal champed her gums like a baby foal and lowered her head. The mare snorted and put her ears back.

'Let her go,' Lawson whispered.

'No way!' Jess hissed. She gave another tug. But Opal clambered the rest of the way up the ramp and into the truck, yanking the rope through Jess's hand and giving her a scorching burn. Jess mouthed a few choice words and shook her hand, trying to lessen the pain.

'Told you to let go,' Lawson said.

At that moment, the creamy mare squealed.

Opal clattered back down the ramp, but before she could get out Lawson leaned over and grabbed her by the mane. 'Whoa!' He looked at Jess pleadingly. 'Just a few more seconds.'

Jess held Opal on the ramp, waiting, as Lawson backed away. Within a minute the creamy mare appeared at the gateway.

'Lead her down,' Lawson whispered.

Jess called Opal softly and brought her down the ramp, then walked her briskly to the exit gate.

'Not yet,' called Lawson. 'Wait.'

'Stuff that,' said Jess, reaching for the latch and letting herself through. 'She's done enough.'

Safely inside the forcing yard, Jess exhaled loudly and gave Opal a pat. 'Clever girl!' She looked at Luke. 'Did you see that? How good was she?'

He smiled and nodded towards the yard. 'Look!'

She spun around to see the creamy mare making her way down the ramp, snorting suspiciously. The other horses followed and soon all four were together in the holding yard.

Grace hooted loudly, making them all spook again. 'Way to go, Opal!'

There were more cheers from her friends. Even Lawson was smiling.

But Jess knew it wasn't time to smile yet. It would be a long time before those horses understood that they'd just been saved. She wasn't even sure herself if they *had* been saved, or just drawn further into a world that they clearly didn't want to be a part of.

'I'm going to get some hay for them,' said Grace, running towards the feed shed.

Shara ran after her. 'Wait for me!'

Jess felt Luke's arm slip around her waist. 'Thanks, Jessy.'

She looked up at him. 'They are some seriously

messed-up horses, Luke. What are you guys going to do with them?'

'Tame them.' He gave her a comical look that was laced with uncertainty. 'Somehow . . .'

'Do you think that's even possible?' She watched the four brumbies slamming up against each other in the corner of the yard. 'How are you *ever* going to convince them that humans are their friends after what they've been through? Horses never forget bad treatment. It just seems . . . like mission impossible.'

'That's the sad part,' said Luke. 'It's *not* if you trap them properly. You'll see when we get the next lot.'

'The *next* lot?' said Jess, horrified. 'You mean there are *more*?'

'Only another six,' said Luke. 'Lawson bought them.'

'*Only* . . . another six? Are you guys crazy?'

3

'THESE ONES WERE passively trapped using salt and molasses,' Luke explained as he took her by the hand and led her to the front gate. 'They're totally different. You're gonna love these guys.'

Jess heard the rumbling engine of another large vehicle. Around a bend in the road came a truck driven by Lawson's friend Bob, wearing a big wide smile and a black hat.

'Lawson and I started handling these ones,' said Luke, as Lawson drove his truck away from the loading ramp, making way for the other to be backed in. 'We can even get halters on some of them, and pick up their feet. The younger ones are the easiest.' Suddenly he was glowing with the satisfaction that Jess always saw in him when he talked about handling young horses.

The truck stopped at the loading ramp and Bob jumped out. His jeans were rolled up past his ankles and his feet were bare. He gave Jess a friendly nod. 'Got some nice types in there,' he said. 'Make good station horses most of 'em.' He grinned. 'Maybe it's time you got a young one and sold old Dodger to me.'

'Nice try, Bob,' Jess laughed. He'd been angling to buy Dodger for years.

'I'd give you fifty bucks for him,' said Lawson, striding past. 'He's not worth more than that.'

Jess snorted.

'She drives a hard bargain, Bob, trust me on that one,' Lawson said, putting a hand on the man's shoulder. 'Come up for a cuppa before you head off, hey?'

Bob nodded and the two men walked to the house.

'You guys right unloading them?' Lawson called over his shoulder.

'Yep!' Luke wrenched the back door open and one by one the horses clattered and slid down the loading ramp, some calmly, others like lunatics. They were mostly chestnuts and bays, all surprisingly stout, with thick manes and winter coats.

Jess felt enormously relieved as they trotted through the gates out into the campdraft arena and cantered in a great swirling mass of tossing manes and feathered legs. At least these ones weren't injured.

'Let's get them something to eat,' said Luke.

Jess helped Luke carry bales of hay from the feed

17

shed, then split them and throw them around the arena. The brumbies quickly settled into feeding. As they ate, Luke slipped in through the arena gate.

'Are you sure you should go in there?' asked Jess, hovering at the gateway.

'Sure.' Luke walked slowly towards a pale chestnut of about fourteen hands, and lowered himself onto one heel, making himself small in front of the horse. It lifted its head and stopped chewing, a clump of hay hanging from its mouth.

Luke stayed motionless as the horse stretched its nose towards him. It took a step forward and sniffed. Jess smiled as it ran its nose up the side of his arm and smeared green hay slobber over his shirt.

Luke rubbed the horse's cheek, then slowly stood. It resumed chewing while he rubbed it all over with circular, rhythmic motions. Soon the horse curled its lip in pleasure and Luke grinned as he scratched around its belly.

'You *have* been handling them,' Jess said, impressed.

'Hasn't taken long,' he said. 'Two weeks. Some of the older ones aren't so friendly but this guy loves me. I called him Buddy.' Luke ran a hand over the small horse's back. 'Cos that's what you've been, haven't you? You've been my buddy.' The horse dropped its head and took another mouthful of hay.

'Come in and meet them,' Luke said to her.

Jess joined him. A tall bay colt shied and darted to the opposite side of the arena, taking the others with him, but as they settled again, Luke moved closer to another chestnut. He approached calmly and ran a hand over the horse's shoulder, repeating the rubbing and scratching until he was picking up its feet and running his hands around its head and ears. The horse let out a long sigh.

Jess noted the size and stockiness of the horse. It was well put together, not at all like the melon-headed, ewe-necked brumbies she'd heard about.

'That's a really nice horse,' she said, surprised.

'It is, ay,' said Luke, still rubbing and scratching.

'I thought they'd be ugly.'

'Not the tablelands brumbies. There have been some good stallions introduced to their herds over the years, real good ones, and these guys have been trapped and carefully handled. We shouldn't have any trouble re-homing most of them.'

Luke kept talking as he walked through the herd and Jess marvelled at the way he moved among them, knowing when to approach, when to retreat, how to put their wild souls at ease. He had less success with a couple of older mares, who eyed him warily and turned their hind-quarters at him, but he let them be, focusing on the younger, more receptive ones.

'Can I come in too?' said a small voice from the side-lines. It was Grace, peering through two lower rails.

Luke hesitated. 'All right, pat Buddy,' he said, nodding towards the little horse. 'I've gotta go and unpack anyway.'

Grace joined Jess in the arena and together they moved slowly and carefully among the brumbies, eventually turning some buckets upside-down and sitting side by side, just watching them.

'Where'd Shara go?' asked Jess.

'To the movies with Corey.'

Jess nodded. 'Not tempted by any of these fine steeds?'

'Nah, but I'll help re-home them,' said Grace. 'I might ask Lawson if I can start that bay colt. I'd want a cut of the sale price, though. He'd get good money for him.'

'You sound like a horse dealer.'

Grace shrugged. 'When my dream horse does come along, I want to be able to afford him.'

'What about Luke's mob?' said Jess.

Grace arched both eyebrows. 'I don't know what Luke's gonna do with that lot.'

Jess looked at the four bewildered horses, slamming up against each other in the nearby yard. 'Nor do I,' she said.

Later in the afternoon, Jess found Luke sitting under the big coachwood tree near the round yard, staring at his mob of four brumbies. They were wild animals that had once galloped with the wind, knowing nothing but hundreds of kilometres of unfenced mountain scrub, deep ravines and trickling creeks, relying on fitness and speed for survival. Now they milled around in the muddy confines of a stockyard.

She sat next to him. 'You okay?'

'Yeah, just sitting here thinking.' He looked at her. 'How good would it be to build a brumby sanctuary? We could rescue more horses like these.'

Jess resisted the temptation to make loud choking noises. 'So how come you ended up with this lot and Lawson ended up with the others?' she asked.

'Lawson said these ones were too far gone. But I just couldn't leave them. I know I can turn them around.' He looked at her suddenly with an earnest expression. 'I was kinda hoping you would help me.'

'How?'

'Come and work with me, properly, you know, like full-time.'

Jess laughed. That was ridiculous. 'I can't, I go to school, remember?'

'So quit.'

'Quit school?'

'Yeah. I did it.' He took her hand and squeezed it. 'We could re-home wild horses; stop them becoming pet food.'

'My parents wouldn't let me. They'd freak.'

'Can't they see how amazing you are with horses?' He paused. 'If you could do absolutely anything for a job, what would you do?'

'Train horses.'

'See?' He shrugged. 'How will school help you with that?'

'But . . .' The idea of an education had been drilled into Jess's psyche for as long as she could remember. The plan had always been to go to uni. 'What would I say to Mum and Dad?'

'Just talk to them, they'll understand.'

But Jess wasn't as confident. 'How would we afford to pay for all the feed and everything?'

'Don't worry about that,' he said. 'I've got it covered.'

'But it's going to cost a heap to feed them and vet them. That colt needs gelding. They're all injured. They need worming and vaccinating . . .' A huge list of bills was building in her head. 'How come you could buy these brumbies in the first place? What happened about your dad? You were going to try to find him while you were down at Mathews' Flat. Why were you away for so long?'

Luke plucked at a piece of grass in front of him, hesitating. 'My dad's dead. He died of cancer six months ago. I already knew before I left to get the brumbies.'

'Hey?'

'We stopped in at Armidale on the way,' Luke continued, 'went to a solicitor, to sort out my father's will. Turns out he left me everything he had: a property at Mathews' Flat and a bit of money. It wasn't a lot. I used some of it to buy the brumbies.'

Jess looked at him, stunned. Luke owned a property in Mathews' Flat? That was miles away, interstate in fact – not even in Queensland!

'Lawson wanted me to put all the money in the bank, lock it up for years in some account and do nothing with it. But finding those brumbies was like some weird sort of calling. It was just too much of a coincidence that they were from Mathews' Flat.' He shrugged. 'I felt a really strong connection with them.'

'And you got a property? You mean, like a house?'

'Yeah, with forty hectares of land. It was my father's place,' said Luke. 'He's buried in the cemetery nearby. So is my mum.' He looked at her with troubled eyes. 'It's where I was born.'

So, it was like . . . home . . . to him?

Luke never spoke much about his childhood, but Jess knew it had been all over the place and mostly unhappy. His mum had died when he was two, then his father adopted him out when he was four. He'd lived with several foster families before he finally came to Harry and Annie's place.

'Did you go and look at it?'

He shook his head. 'Not yet. I will when I'm ready. But I want to do something about these brumbies first.' He stood up and held out a hand for her. 'Speaking of which, the vet's here.'

Jess followed him back to the yards, her head spinning like a flywheel.

By the time all the brumbies had been vetted and assessed, it was nearly dark.

Luke's brumbies were pushed into the cattle crush and sedated with a dart gun so John Duggin could stitch wounds and generally patch them up. It was a horrible process which Jess found almost as distressing as the brumbies did.

Sapphire, the creamy stallion, had to be knocked out cold so that John could clean and stitch the gaping wound on the horse's face.

Sapphire was left in the big arena to slowly wake, with his herd standing groggily nearby. When he did, he seemed more traumatised than before, and charged around, roaring at the other horses through the fence.

'Should just put him down,' said Lawson, watching from the sidelines. 'It's cruel keeping him alive.'

But Luke refused. John sedated the stallion again in case he broke his stitches, and those of his mares, and left them to it.

Jess walked back to the stables. The night-time sounds of bats and possums mingling with whinnying brumbies, clinking gates and friendly and familiar voices made her smile. For some reason, she always seemed to feel happiest when she was utterly knackered.

'Do you need a lift home?' asked Grace, wandering up behind her. 'Lawson said he's leaving in ten minutes.'

'That would be great,' said Jess. 'Don't fancy riding home in the dark. I just want to say goodnight to Luke and then I'll come up.'

Luke was sweeping the stable aisle with a big, wide broom, making long swishing noises that echoed against the quiet night. The feedroom was closed and locked and the horses were quiet except for an occasional sleepy snort. He propped the broom up against a wall when he saw Jess.

He put his arms around her shoulders and breathed into her hair, making a big warm cocoon around her that she wanted to stay curled up inside forever.

'You're like one of those therapy pets,' he said. 'You know, the ones they take around to old people's homes.'

'You calling me a dog?'

'An old Labrador,' he said teasingly. 'A nice one, though, a girl one, one that gets washed a lot.'

'Thanks,' she grumbled. 'Hey, I'm really sorry you didn't get a chance to meet your dad.'

Luke sighed. 'So weird. I always thought once I was eighteen I would just look him up and find out what happened, but I never imagined he wouldn't be there.'

He looked into the yard, where the brumby stallion still paced frenetically. 'I'll be all right, though. So will that stallion, once he gets used to the idea.' He looked at her happily. 'You and me, Jessy. We'll sort them out.'

Jess gave an awkward laugh. Surely he didn't really expect her to just drop out of school?

4

THAT NIGHT JESS lay on her bed and gazed at the ceiling. She pulled out her phone and stared at Luke's photo for a while. Then she messaged Shara.

> I want to leave school.
>
> **Huh? Why?**
>
> I want to work with Luke and brumbies.
>
> **Don't be insane. You're too brainy.**
>
> Mum probably wouldn't let me anyway.

Within seconds her phone rang. 'What's going on?' said Shara.

'Luke wants me to leave school and work with him full-time.'

'Yeah, right,' said Shara. 'And who's gonna pay you? Isn't he supposed to be doing a farrier's apprenticeship?'

'He could still do that.'

'What about you? You wouldn't earn any money.'

'I don't care about money. Some things are more important than money, Sharsy. '

'Yeah, like an education. Surely you're not serious, Jess.'

Jess groaned. 'School gets in the way of *everything*!'

Shara laughed. '*Horses* get in the way of everything. So do boyfriends. Corey is the biggest distraction. I don't know how I'll ever become a vet with him hanging around. But seriously, Jess. Don't go blowing off school for something that can wait.'

'But it can't wait. Luke needs me now and so do the brumbies.' She told Shara about Luke's father and his inheritance: the property in the tablelands of New South Wales. 'What if he wants to move down there, Shara?'

'So *that's* what this is about,' said her bestie. 'He wouldn't leave you, would he?'

'I don't know.'

'Nah,' said Shara, brushing it off. 'Luke would never move away from Coachwood Crossing. It's his home. He loves it here. And he's totally crazy about you.'

'Maybe I could just take a gap year,' said Jess, wishing she could feel as confident as Shara. 'Everyone takes a gap year.'

'Everyone takes a gap year *after* Year Twelve, and I was kinda hoping to spend *my* gap year with *you*!'

Jess was silent.

'Jess, you can't give up your whole life just because you're scared Luke will leave you. That's insane.' Shara changed to her feminist career-woman tone. 'Get a bit of guts about you, Jessica Fairley. A woman's destiny must be her own!'

'What if my destiny is to be *on* my own?' said Jess glumly.

'Je-e-ss!' Her mum called from the kitchen. 'Dinner's ready!'

'I gotta go,' said Jess. 'I'll see you tomorrow.'

Jess sat at the dinner table and stared at the spinach ravioli without any appetite.

Caroline untied her apron and joined Jess and Craig at the table. 'Good to use up some of the spinach from the garden,' she said cheerfully. 'Full of iron and folic acid. We'll have to put more sawdust around the plants, Craig. Slow those snails down a bit.'

Jess stared into her dinner, deep in thought.

'Eat up, Jess,' said Caroline.

Jess poked at the food with her fork.

Caroline took hold of the salad servers, plucked out some radicchio leaves and passed the salad bowl to Jess. She pushed it on to her dad without looking up.

Jess could feel her dad's gaze moving between herself and her mother.

Caroline put her knife and fork down and took a calming breath. 'What's wrong, Jessica?'

'I've been thinking about my career,' said Jess. 'I hate working in the bakery.'

'Good. I'm glad you do,' said Craig. 'You might aspire to something a bit more challenging.'

'Brumbies are challenging.'

'And they're very worthwhile, but they're not a career.'

Jess slumped.

'I heard about Luke's inheritance,' said her dad.

'Who told you?' Again, Jess felt miffed that she hadn't been the first to know.

'Annie talked to Caroline about it.'

'He wants to build a brumby sanctuary and re-home horses.'

'And he wants you to join him?'

Jess nodded.

Craig let out a deep sigh and put his hand on Jess's. 'I think it's great that he's so passionate about something. But don't throw your own dreams away for the sake of someone else's, honey. Someone who loves you would never ask you to do that.'

'But Luke's dreams are my dreams too.'

'Are you sure about that? Because once you throw your education away, your goals will be so much harder to reach. Think about your whole life, Jess. Not just about tomorrow. Not just about Luke.'

'You guys always criticise Luke.'

'We do *not*,' said her dad defensively. 'We like Luke a lot. But he is who he is.'

'What's *that* supposed to mean?'

'It means just that. He has his plans and you have yours. If they go hand-in-hand that's great.' He gave her arm a pat. 'Build your own dreams, Jess. Don't just ride on the tails of someone else's.'

That night Jess slept restlessly. Outside, the wind shook the leathery leaves of the coachwood trees and scraped their branches across the roof. Her dreams were filled with the sound of hooves stampeding over darkened mountains. She woke, her mind unsettled by images of Luke standing on a mountain property in another state.

A soft tapping noise broke through the sound of the trees. She sat up and squinted into the darkness. Someone was at her window.

'Luke?' Jess hurriedly undid the catch at the top of the window and slid it up. 'What are you doing here?'

'I couldn't sleep,' he whispered, leaning into the window and climbing in headfirst.

Jess grabbed him by the waist and hauled him in, giggling and shushing. He landed like a lump, on top of her. His clothes were damp and grimy. 'Shhhhhhh!' She shoved him off her.

'Turn the light on,' he whispered.

'No, it'll wake my parents!' Instead, she groped around for a small torch in her bedside drawer. She pulled the doona over both their heads and switched the torch on. They huddled together, the covers like a little teepee, with streaks and shadows making their faces look distorted.

He chuckled. 'You look funny.'

'You look like a homeless person. You smell like one too.'

'Kiss me anyway.'

'No,' she laughed and shoved him off. He toppled over backwards and landed on the wooden floorboards with a thump.

She heard a light click on down the hallway and her mother's voice. 'Jessica?'

Luke looked at her, terror-stricken, and commando-crawled under her bed.

'It's only me, Mum, I fell out of bed,' she called back, barely managing to suppress her laughter.

'You okay?' asked her mum in a sleepy voice.

'Yeah,' she called back.

Then she hung her head upside-down and peered

under the bed, shining the torchlight onto Luke's face. He looked ready to explode with laughter.

'What are you *doing* here?'

'I needed a therapy pet.'

'You need therapy full stop,' she said. 'You're crazy.'

'I'm crazy about you.' He wriggled towards her. 'Just one kiss,' he said, twisting his head sideways and pressing his lips to hers. 'One kiss and I'll go away.'

She kissed him upside-down, her lips and chin and nose all not where they were supposed to be. But she liked the weirdness of it. 'Where will you go?'

'Oh, I'll just curl up under a tree somewhere, I suppose. In the cold. And the rain. I'll just *pretend* that some-body . . . somewhere . . . loves me.'

'Nawww . . .'

Luke pulled a sad face and she slithered off the bed. He rolled out from under it and Jess pulled him onto the small woollen rug, wrapped her arms around his neck and kissed him properly. He put his arms around her and hugged her, burying his face in her neck and exhaling.

'I can't leave school,' she whispered.

'I know,' he whispered back.

'Are you going to move away?'

He didn't answer, but something about the way he held her made her fears grow. This place, this property, was really tugging at him.

She held him like that for ages, until she heard the breezy whistle of pre-snores.

'Don't fall asleep here,' she whispered. 'You can sleep on the balcony, on the big futon. Mum and Dad won't mind.'

She found him some blankets, helped him back out the window and heard him tiptoe around the balcony to the front verandah. She rolled back into bed, wrapping her arms tightly around herself, and listened to the wind outside. Beneath its creaks and moans she sensed the almost whispered rhythm of galloping hooves, far, far away, belonging almost to another time.

She shuddered and shook it off. Weird what wind could bring, or make you imagine.

'Look what the cat dragged in,' said Craig when Jess walked into the kitchen the next morning. Luke sat across from him at the table, his hair wet from the shower. 'I found him on the futon out the front. Thought he was some old dero.'

Luke grinned up at her from an overflowing bowl of Weet-Bix.

'Morning,' Jess smiled, not bothering to conjure up surprise. She liked the way Luke looked in her kitchen.

She ignored her dad's suspicious eyes darting between the two of them and walked over to Luke, put her arms around his shoulders and kissed him on the cheek.

'Hi, gorgeous,' Luke mumbled through his breakfast.

Craig frowned. Jess gave him a hug too.

Luke finished his cereal and took the bowl to the sink. 'See you at Harry's?'

She nodded. Within moments the front door clicked and he was gone.

Jess smiled to herself. It would take more than some patch of dirt in New South Wales to come between her and Luke Matheson. She'd been demented to even imagine it.

She noticed her dad staring at her with a worried frown.

'It's okay, I'm not going to run away with him,' she said, emptying the last of the Weet-Bix crumbs into a bowl. 'You don't have to worry.'

Her dad looked relieved.

'I do want to work with the brumbies, though.'

'I wish school rated as highly as the brumbies,' said Craig.

'It does, Dad. I want to do both.'

'You *can* do both,' said Caroline, entering the kitchen in a batik robe. 'But school has to come first. Once home-work's done, you can use all your spare time to work with

Luke.' She took the kettle from the stove and began filling it at the sink.

'All of it?'

Her mum replaced the kettle and lit the stove. 'How much of *all of it* do you mean?'

'I mean *all* of it,' said Jess. 'Stay there on weekends. So I can start really early in the mornings.'

Caroline paused. 'What do you think, Craig?'

'I would stay at the house, with Annie,' Jess added.

'So, you wouldn't want to move in with Luke or anything?' asked her dad.

'No.'

'Good, because I don't think . . .'

Jess held up her hand. She hated those talks. 'It's okay, guys. We're not . . . you know . . .'

Both Caroline and Craig looked relieved.

Jess blushed. *Gawd. How embarrassing*. As if she wanted her parents to know about *that*.

'If your schoolwork is done, to a high standard – to your best – then you can stay there as much as you genuinely need to,' said Caroline. She gave a small sniff, putting one hand on Jess's shoulder. 'You're just . . . growing up so much.'

'You're gonna come and see them, aren't you?'

'The brumbies? Of course.'

'I'll be busy,' said Jess, scooping the last of breakfast out of her bowl. 'I'll be needing power food.'

'Well, that I can help you with!' said Caroline, sounding pleased.

Jess was relieved. It was a great arrangement, one that would help Luke and his wild horses but also help her follow her own destiny. She couldn't wait to get to work. She couldn't wait to tell Luke!

5

WHEN JESS RODE through Harry's front gate later that morning, Lawson's brumbies seemed to be settling well. Jess stabled Dodger and Opal and joined her friends at the yards. She took a moment to watch how the wildies interacted with each other, so unlike the domestic horses. They moved about the yards as one, a mob. Some were shorter, some taller, but they were all cut from the same stuff, with identical white-striped faces, and behaved as though they had the same thoughts pulsing through their minds. If one startled, they all startled. If one looked to the left, the others did likewise. They all stood facing the road, or they all stood facing the stables. One might wander a short distance away and get a drink from the trough but it would then return to the mob and face the same direction as the others.

Grace was in the round yard, working with the bay

colt. She walked behind, driving him forward with a gentle flick of her rope. The horse stopped and swung his tail at her, ears flat back, and she calmly drove him on again. Every time the horse stopped and swung his tail, Grace clicked him up again.

After several minutes, more stops and more flicks of the rope, the colt turned its face towards Grace. Jess smiled. She had watched this process dozens of times with Biyanga's youngsters. 'Joining up', 'hooking up', 'latching on', 'shadowing' – different trainers called it different things, but it was always magic to watch. Jess stood there, entranced, watching for the signs, waiting for the magic to happen. Grace turned her shoulder to the colt.

'He's coming,' Jess mouthed. Grace winked while the horse walked cautiously towards her with an outstretched nose. She stood dead still. The horse took another tentative step and placed its nose on her shoulder, then snuffled up and knocked her cap off, eyeing it curiously as it fell to the ground. Grace was trying to hold back a chuckle.

Jess left her with the colt and found Luke in the arena with the pale chestnut, Buddy. He slid his hand down behind the back of the little horse's fetlock and picked up its foot. He held it for a moment and then placed it back on the ground, running his hand back up the horse's leg and patting him on the shoulder.

'He doesn't seem to mind that,' she said.

Luke left the rope dangling from Buddy's halter and walked over to Jess.

'So how are your brumbies going?' she asked. 'Are you going to start handling them too?'

'The stallion's not too good. Nor are his mares. I need to move them out to clean the yards, but they go nuts every time I go near the gate.'

'Are they eating? Drinking?'

He shrugged. 'Not really.'

'Do you want some help from Opal?'

'That'd be good.'

Jess went and got her from the stables while Luke finished with Buddy.

'See if you can get her to lead them into another yard while I clean out the old one,' said Luke.

Jess led Opal in and out of the yards and the injured brumbies followed tentatively behind.

'She's a natural at coaching,' said Luke from the sidelines. 'She really seems to understand the job.'

Jess smiled and nodded as she tied Opal by the gate. The filly just had a way about her that seemed to calm and reassure their flighty nerves. 'I think she's enjoying it too.'

She helped Luke muck out the yard. When it was clean, Opal brought the brumbies back in, introduced them to biscuits of fresh grassy hay and showed them that the dry, wispy stems were good to eat. The two mares and the buckskin foal nibbled tentatively, but the stallion stood, tight-lipped, with his ears back, still refusing to eat. His blue eyes darted nervously at every small noise or movement. He looked gaunt, hollow-flanked, with sunken eyes. But his head was still high, tense, and braced against this new world.

'Sapphire's going to take more time than the others,' said Luke.

'Getting the mares to eat is a start,' Jess answered. 'Hopefully he'll follow their lead.'

Jess watched the two mares, standing with their sides touching, then looked proudly at Opal. What her secret was Jess didn't know, but having Opal around somehow gave Jess hope that with persistence and patience, maybe these wildies *could* form a bond with humans.

By Friday afternoon, Jess was well on top of her study and ready to work the entire weekend with the brumbies. Grace and Rosie would both come and help too. The three of them planned to sleep in the spare room at Annie's.

Jess spent the afternoon grooming Buddy while Luke tried to catch and halter some of the others. But his mind didn't seem to be on the job. He appeared to be lost in his own thoughts.

That night, as she drifted towards sleep, Jess was stirred by a hissing sound.

'Jessy, psst. Jess!' Luke peered through the bedroom door. 'Jess,' he whispered again.

'Go away,' Grace grumbled at him. 'Or I'll tell Annie you're in here.'

'Shut up, Grace,' he shot back at her. 'I'll tell Annie you snuck out with Elliot last night.'

Grace sat bolt upright. 'I did not!'

'I didn't know you snuck out with Elliot.' Jess squinted into the dark room.

'That's because I *didn't*!' hissed Grace.

'It'll be your word against mine,' chuckled Luke.

'Get out of here!' Grace hurled her pillow at the door.

Jess flipped her quilt off. 'What's the matter?' She stumbled into the hallway and closed the door behind her.

Luke was already sitting at the dining-room table in front of a laptop. 'I just got an email from a lady at a brumby rescue group and she said there've been more.'

'More what?'

'More tablelands brumbies put through the sales. Stallions, mostly. They're always creamy and they're always scarred. It's been happening for months. Someone's systematically running them, Jess.'

'Isn't that illegal?'

'*Totally*,' said Luke. 'But no one seems able to stop them.' He chewed at an already short fingernail.

'Well, there's nothing you can do about it now. Time to stop worrying – go and sit on the couch,' Jess ordered, closing the laptop.

She went to the linen cupboard and grabbed a blanket, then returned to find him lying on the couch with his hands behind his head. She threw the blanket over him and snuggled in alongside.

He wrapped his arms around her. She could feel the cool moonstone that always hung around his neck on a worn leather strap that had been replaced several times.

'These people are going to wipe them out if they keep catching all the stallions,' mumbled Luke quietly.

'They've already been wiped out,' said Jess. 'The national parks people have already massacred most of the herds in the tablelands. They shot them from helicopters.' The Guy Fawkes massacre – when six hundred wild horses were shot in the middle of the foaling season, their carcasses left to rot – had been well publicised.

'I reckon there are more, Jess. Ones they don't know about.' Luke paused. 'When I was really little, I used to hear brumbies at night, their hoofbeats.'

'Wow, that would have been cool.'

'I've never forgotten them. My father reckoned they were ghosts. He called them Saladin's spirits.'

'I've heard of Saladin,' said Jess. More than a hundred years ago, a creamy stallion of that name had been crossed with a thoroughbred. The descendants formed a foundation sire for the stockhorses, but many also ran wild in the gorge country of the New South Wales tablelands. They had creamy genes, and some had blue eyes.

Luke was quiet for a while. 'Mum called them the night raiders. The stallions would come at night for the mares. One took her best horse, Stormy-girl. She used to write stories about her, living with the wild horses. After mum died, her best friend used to read the stories to me.'

Luke lingered on that thought a moment longer before continuing. 'I remember seeing Stormy-girl and the wild stallion outside my bedroom window. She was a coloured mare, you could see her white patches moving in the dark.' Luke turned to Jess. 'We lived at the bottom of a big mountain.'

'Really?'

'I don't know,' he said, sounding suddenly muddled. 'I don't know if it was a dream or if it was real.'

'You must have been pretty young.'

'I was only four.'

Jess lay in Luke's arms, imagining a mare called Stormy-girl galloping through the trees with a wild brumby stallion. 'Did she ever go looking for her? Try to get her back?'

'Yeah,' said Luke quietly. 'In Mum's stories there was a place.' His voice took on a story-telling tone. 'There's a place on the tablelands where all the boundaries meet, a no-man's land where wild horses live.' He smiled fondly, as though filled with good memories. 'That's how her stories always started.'

'Go on,' whispered Jess.

'In a landlocked valley, wild and unclaimed, Saladin's spirit is born to the blue-eyed brumbies. The place is so exquisitely special, it must be kept secret.'

He laughed suddenly. 'I'm being stupid.'

'No, no, go on. It's a good story.'

'She called it Brumby Mountain,' Luke continued. 'She told me it was real. I can't remember much more.' He paused and his voice changed again. 'I know it's really stupid, but I've got it in my head that that's where these brumbies are coming from. They've got the blue eyes. They're creamy like Saladin. People wouldn't get away with brumby-running in the national parks these days. So where are the runners catching these horses?'

'So you think there might be a breakaway mob, hiding out somewhere, that the parks don't know about?'

'Sounds crazy, doesn't it?' said Luke.

'Not really,' Jess said. 'If only they could tell us. If only Sapphire could talk.'

Luke sighed. 'Sapphire.'

Jess didn't answer. She didn't need to point out what a mess the horse was.

'I did the wrong thing, trying to save him. I've just made him suffer more.'

Jess leaned over and flicked off the lamp. 'Get some sleep.'

She snuggled into his arms but he barely hugged her back. She could almost hear him thinking. Again, she could feel the pull that the horses, the mountain, the property, were having over him.

The next morning the front door slammed and Lawson walked into the lounge room. 'Your dad's outside, Jessica. He just pulled up in the driveway.'

Luke exploded off the couch, sending Jess sprawling to the floor with the blanket wrapped around her head. She hurriedly pulled it off and jumped to her feet, checking that her pyjamas were where they were supposed to be.

Lawson roared with laughter.

'Pig,' she muttered.

Luke mumbled a few curses and flopped back onto the couch.

'Hey, I just got a phone call from a bloke called Frank O'Brien,' said Lawson, using his toe to peel off a boot, then kicking it into a shoe basket by the front door. 'He does horse starting clinics with teenagers. He's coming out to have a look at my brumbies tomorrow afternoon. He needs some young ones for a workshop that's coming up in a few weeks.'

'Oh, that's fantastic,' said Jess. 'Your brumbies would be perfect.'

'He said as long as they can lead and tie up, he'll take them,' said Lawson.

'That shouldn't be too hard,' said Luke. 'Yours are just about ready to go.' He sighed. 'My ones are just nuts, though. I can't get anywhere near them yet.'

'Still haven't settled?' asked Lawson.

Luke pulled a face and shook his head. 'Nup.'

Lawson walked to the kitchen, and Jess followed. Annie already had a big pot of tea steeping, a mountain of toast and some sausages and eggs sizzling in a pan. Jess's home-grown asparagus sat on top, warming. It had become the new breakfast tradition.

'You two looked sweet cuddled up on the couch like that,' Annie said, rolling some sausages over with the

47

tongs. 'You reminded me of me and Harry years ago. We used to snog for hours.'

'Told you she'd be cool,' said Luke in Jess's ear. 'I'm going down to the flat. See you later.'

Jess poured herself a mug of tea and squirted some honey into it. 'He's stressed out about the brumbies,' she said to Annie. 'He couldn't sleep.'

'He's always been a bit like that. Can't keep still for long,' Annie answered. 'He used to have nightmares when he was younger.'

'Yeah, he told me.'

'We used to find him fast asleep in Biyanga's stable in the mornings, all curled up in the wood shavings around the stallion's feet. He used to sneak out the bedroom window, through the courtyard and down to the stables. He said the sounds of the horses made him sleep.'

'And when the horses don't sleep, he doesn't either.'

'Something like that,' smiled Annie. She paused and looked thoughtful. 'But especially so with these ones, I think. They're from the same country as him. Luke was born in the tablelands. He has the same mountain spirit running through his veins as that old stallion. There's a connection there, somehow.'

The front door swung open again and Grace's mum, in holey tracky-dacks and a flannelette shirt, kicked off a pair of steel-capped boots as she entered. 'Hey, Annie,' she called out in her blokey voice. She walked into the kitchen and gave her sister-in-law a quick hug. 'Came to see the brumbies, but the smell of your cooking got to me.'

'Get yourself a plate, love,' said Annie.

Mrs Arnold helped herself to some sausages and eggs and pulled up a stool at the bench while Annie poured her a mug of tea. 'Grace reckons the stallion's a total nut job.'

'It is. Luke's really upset about it,' said Jess, hoping Mrs Arnold wouldn't go down there and start bullying him around.

'Poor horse,' said Mrs Arnold. 'Brumby-running is a disgusting practice. Bunch of idiots, all galloping around thinking they're the Man from Snowy River, injuring their horses, injuring themselves.' She hacked into a sausage and kept talking. 'The stockmen in Banjo's poem never used a boat winch to haul them onto a truck, they never chained the brumbies to a four-wheel drive and dragged them through the bush. It's a disgrace what goes on these days.'

Jess left Mrs Arnold with Annie and headed down to the yards. Grace was working with the bay colt again.

'Did Lawson tell you about the clinic?' Jess called out.

'Yeah,' Grace called back. 'These guys will be perfect for it. This one is catching on really fast.'

Jess left her to it and went to find Luke. She found him sitting under the coachwood tree with his head in his hands.

Sapphire paced from one end of the yard to another. The stallion was a sad sight, thin and ribby, so dehydrated that his flanks had sunk into his belly.

'Where are his mares?' Jess asked.

'We had to separate him from them,' Luke said glumly. 'He hurt one. He didn't mean it. He was charging at one of the domestic horses and she got in the way.' He sighed heavily. 'I've rung John.'

Jess's heart sank. She sat next to him and rested her head on his shoulder. 'Need a therapy pet?'

He laughed half-heartedly and put an arm around her shoulder.

'You don't have to hang around,' she said. 'Lawson and John will take care of it.'

'I want to be here. It wouldn't be right for me to cop out.'

'Mind if I do?' She had enough bad memories of horses being destroyed without adding to them.

He shook his head.

'Don't do it where his mares can see,' she said quietly.

Jess left Luke at the yards and set about finding jobs to do. She saw John's four-wheel drive pull up at the front gate and made herself busy, trying not to think about what was happening in the stallion's yard. She went to the stables and did a poo patrol, trying to ignore the hum of a backhoe engine and the tractor putting outside. She tried to block out images of the creamy stallion being dragged down the laneway, his feet in chains and head dragging behind. His blue eyes, she knew, would be open and empty as he was thrown into a big hole and then buried forever, away from his mares, away from his mountains. It was too depressing.

Luke didn't come up for lunch. Jess walked down to the stables and knocked on the door of his flat. Fang nudged the door open with his nose and wagged his tail when he saw Jess. The flat was a small square stable with a concrete floor, now converted into a room. A long, bench-style table sectioned off the kitchenette, which had one sink, a toaster oven and a bar fridge with stickers all over it. There was stuff all over the bench – farrier's tools, jumpers, empty soft-drink cans, a few dirty plates and mugs.

A small two-seater couch and an old cable reel with a TV on it were all that could squeeze into the rest of the flat. Luke lay on the couch with his boots hanging over the armrest and his arms around Filth, staring at the wall like a ghost. When Jess came in, the dog gave a single lazy tail-wag and closed his eyes again. Luke hid his face behind Filth's long shaggy body.

'You okay?'

Luke kept his face buried in the dog's chest. He shook his head twice.

'Want some time to yourself?'

He shook his head again. 'I want to go back there.'

'Go back where?'

'To Mathews' Flat. I can't stop thinking about it.'

'About your parents?'

'Yeah, and the property and the horses. All of it. I want to stop whoever's running those brumbies.' He looked up at her suddenly. 'Come with me, Jessy. I don't want to leave you behind this time. I miss you too much. We could throw some hay on the back and take the horses.'

'I can't just take off. I have school and home, horses to take care of and a job – and so do you. What about Lawson? What about all these brumbies?'

'She's right, Luke.' Annie appeared at the doorway of the flat. Judy Arnold stood next to her. 'I'm responsible for Jess while she stays here. I told her parents I'd take care of her.'

Luke looked annoyed. 'Next weekend is a long weekend. I'd have her back in time for school the following Tuesday, I promise!'

Annie shook her head. 'Not without her parents' permission.'

Jess sighed. There was no way her mum and dad would let her take off to another state without an adult. There'd been enough drama about that when she had wanted to go droving last year. It was only when Mrs Arnold had agreed to . . . 'Mrs Arnold!'

Judy Arnold scowled. 'What?'

Jess smiled sweetly. 'Fancy a brumby-spotting holiday?'

6

GRACE'S FACE APPEARED through the tiny window of the flat. 'Brumby-spotting?' She looked at her mum. 'How good would that be, to see them in the wild? Can we go?'

Mrs Arnold looked taken aback. 'Where?'

'I know a place,' said Luke.

'Oh, here we go,' she said, heavy with cynicism. 'I know a place too. In fact I know hundreds of places. Doesn't mean I'm gonna find a brumby.'

'It's in the tablelands. Mathews' Flat.'

Mrs Arnold sighed. 'Where you were born. You want to go back there.'

She looked at Annie.

Annie shrugged. 'Think about it, Judy. It'd be good for Luke to go, connect with his past a bit. I could throw some hay to the horses while he's gone. Lawson would help.'

Mrs Arnold's shoulders dropped resignedly.

Jess grinned. She could feel an adventure coming on.

It seemed to take hours to make all the necessary phone calls. Caroline wanted to speak to everyone: Jess, Luke, Mrs Arnold, Annie and then Jess again. But she finally said yes. 'Let *me* break it to your father,' she said before she hung up. 'And you must take some decent food. I don't want you eating truck-stop garbage all the way there.'

Luke agreed to wait until the next weekend. Grace and Mrs Arnold would follow behind in Mrs Arnold's four-wheel drive. Luke refused point-blank to ride in the car with her or let her tow his horse. 'I want to take my own car,' he insisted.

Luke picked Jess up before daybreak on Saturday morning. Filth and Fang panted happily in the back of the HQ ute. Jess gave them quick pats before she loaded Dodger next to Luke's big black gelding, Legsy, then closed the tail ramp and hugged her parents goodbye.

They drove through Coachwood Crossing and turned south towards the freeway as the sun was rising. A sense of freedom filled Jess and she wondered what the week-end might bring.

A few Ks down the road she noticed there was no four-wheel drive behind them. 'Shouldn't we wait for Mrs A to catch up?' she asked, staring out the back window.

'We can join up with them later. I want to make a detour first.'

'Where to?

'Brisbane sales are on. Won't be long – half an hour, max. You can text her if you like.'

'You didn't tell me about this.' She whacked him on the arm. 'I promised I'd be good!'

He looked at her bag on the seat beside him. 'Your phone got Google?'

Jess groaned. 'Luke, you're hopeless!'

'Look up the sales. See what time they start.'

She pulled her phone from her bag and googled the Brisbane saleyards while Luke drove.

'Bidding starts at eleven a.m. with the yarded horses, which are knackery suspects and unbroken types,' she read off her phone. 'Then riding horses are sold through a ring. Saddlery is at the completion of the horse sales.'

'We've got time,' said Luke, checking his watch.

Jess sent Mrs Arnold a brief text suggesting a time for a rendezvous at the Mathews' Flat Hotel and then turned the phone off so as not to hear her protests.

The saleyards were a sea of steel pipes and stamped concrete. Laneways ran through yard after yard and bridges and ramps crossed overhead, with stockmen and auctioneers yodelling prices and upping the bids. Most horses stood listlessly, a few seemed agitated. There were all types, from magnificent broken-down racing stallions to aged kids' ponies and fluffy miniatures. Some had obvious vices like wind-sucking, others looked completely innocent. Some were in appalling condition.

A small foal in particular looked too young to be away from its mother. It was scrawny, with a wormy belly and too many bones showing. Flies crawled in its ears but it seemed too lethargic to shake its tiny head.

'Probably pick that one up for twenty bucks,' said a grey-faced man as he walked past. 'Hasn't got enough meat on it for the doggers.'

Jess shuddered and was relieved when two women entered the yard and began discussing how to get it home.

People walked in and out of the yards, lifting horses' lips and checking teeth. They poked and prodded, picked up legs and inspected hooves.

Crowds of people crushed around the horse under auction, yelling and nodding and placing their bids. The auctioneer called 'All done' and moved quickly to the next horse.

And then Jess spotted them. Unlike the resigned-looking domestic horses, the brumbies were freaking out. Their nostrils flared as they sniffed warily at new and dangerous smells and they huddled closely together for safety, tense and on edge.

'There they are!' said Luke, heading towards them.

Three horses, unmistakeably wild, whinnied nervously: a brown mare, a skittish brown foal and a deep golden palomino stallion. He was tall with one rolling blue eye and one brown one, beneath a matted forelock. He had the same broad shoulders and back as Sapphire, and Jess could instantly tell that they were related. This one, though, had the sweat marks of a saddle, and missing skin around his neck.

'He's so much like Sapphire,' said Jess. 'He has to be from the same country, from the same bloodlines.'

'Look at his back leg,' said Luke.

Jess ran her eyes over his hindquarters and down to where a flap of skin hung from the horse's lower leg, like an old sock.

'Looks like he's been stretched,' said Luke.

'He's been *what*?'

'They rope the horse's hind leg, stretch it back and tie it to a tree. Then they get on and off him. If he moves, he falls over. And if he struggles too much, well . . .' He gestured to the horse's hind leg.

'Contractor brumby-catchers wouldn't bother doing that. Someone's doing this for sport.' Jess turned to Luke. 'Don't the authorities stop this sort of thing?'

'They'll say it happened in transport,' said Luke. 'Wild horses hurt themselves in trucks all the time. It's hard to police.'

The bidding for the brumbies didn't take long. Only one person raised a hand and Jess guessed he was from the knackery. The animals' lives were traded in for a mere fifty bucks. There was some hand-slapping, a nod, and the auctioneers moved on.

Luke had walked away. Jess found him by the carpark, sitting on a patch of grass with his elbows on his knees, tapping a stick on his boot. 'You okay?' she asked.

He nodded.

'We couldn't take them home, there's no room. We couldn't . . .'

He gestured for her to stop. 'It's okay. They're better off, especially the stallion.'

'The foal . . .'

'They were a job lot.'

They sat there in silence, listening to the auctioneer in the distance. Suddenly Luke was on his feet, striding towards a small brick building with *Office* written above the door.

'Where are you going?'

'Gonna find out where they came from.' He disappeared into the building.

Jess didn't follow. Beyond Luke an unmarked truck with a dirty olive-green crate on the back pulled in and Jess watched as several horses were loaded onto the back. Once full, the truck made its way through the carpark and towards the exit gates. Through the gap between the lower horizontal panels, one ice-blue eye stared at her as the truck rolled past. It was the sort of look that would haunt a person in their dreams.

Luke emerged from the office moments later. 'All they know is that they're from New South Wales. They wouldn't tell me any more.'

'At least we know we're headed in the right direction,' said Jess.

Luke was already marching to the car, keys jingling in his hand. They rejoined the highway and headed for the tablelands.

They drove through the city limits and on into the afternoon, with the sun streaming through the window and country music twanging in the cabin. As they travelled up the steep sides of a valley, the road became pitted and potholed and the going slow. The HQ struggled to pull the two horses up the hills and the brakes smoked as it rolled down the other side.

'Dingo!' Luke hit the brakes and slowed. 'What have *you* been up to?' he said as the blocky yellow animal stopped on the side of the road and stared at them.

On the back of the ute, Filth and Fang went nuts, growling and barking, nearly flipping themselves inside-out on their chains. The dingo eyed them briefly and slunk away, its thick bushy tail swallowed up by a fold in the land.

'Must have been after those lambs,' said Jess, pointing to the sheep on the other side of the road.

As they drove into steeper country, the road wound around bends and cut through hillsides. A red-and-white poster strapped to trees became a recurring sight.

1080
WILD
DOG
POISON
Laid on this
property

They saw an enormous dead dog hanging by its two back feet from a star picket. Its tongue was black and shrivelled.

On the back Filth and Fang whined, and Jess caught the rotten smell of it as it wafted through her open window. She cringed. 'Maybe we shouldn't have brought the dogs with us.'

'I was just thinking that,' said Luke quietly. 'Might not be real welcome around here.'

They drove through two more small towns before the

road flattened out again and they came to a small inter-section. One road led to a concrete river crossing, the other to a small cluster of cream-painted tin buildings. HOTEL was painted across the roof of one, MATTY'S FLAT POST OFFICE was scrawled across another. Out the front of the post office was a prehistoric-looking petrol bowser.

Luke let the ute roll to a stop next to it and cut the engine. Jess got out to stretch her legs and was shocked by the dry, cold air. It had a hardness to it she had never felt before. As she opened the front door to the horse float to check on Dodger and Legsy, a middle-aged man in coveralls came to the door of the post office and eyed them suspiciously.

'This thing work?' asked Luke, nodding towards the bowser.

The man didn't answer but ran his eyes to the back of the ute where Filth and Fang panted, tongues out. 'They dingo hybrids, mate?'

'Nah, nah,' said Luke without missing a beat. 'These are pure-breds, Mount Isa Shepherds.' He gave Filth a rub behind the ears. 'A new breed from up north, bred to protect sheep.'

'Oh right,' said the man doubtfully. 'Got big jaws for shepherds.'

'Yeah, that's for killing foxes. They do that too. They

do look a bit like dingos, though, ay,' said Luke, sounding overly jovial.

The man raised an eyebrow.

'Nah, nothin' like them, totally different breeding. These guys won't touch your stock.' Luke pointed to the tray of the ute and signalled for Filth to lie down. The big dog obliged, rolling onto his back and growling playfully.

'They look well-fed enough,' said the man, still not sounding entirely convinced. 'You see they stay that way.'

Luke winked and reached for the petrol spout.

'Where are we staying?' asked Jess, remembering that they had only one flimsy swag between them. The western sky was going a pale pinky cream and the sun was quickly disappearing behind a mound of hills. She could feel the temperature dropping rapidly. 'What'll we do with the horses overnight?'

Luke didn't answer. He finished with the petrol spout and clunked it back onto the bowser.

'Should we book into the hotel?'

'Not yet.' After paying the man, and getting some directions, Luke stepped back into the ute.

'Now where are we going?' asked Jess as she climbed in the other side.

'I want to find the property,' said Luke. 'Before Mrs Arnold gets here. I don't want her hassling me.'

He pulled away from the post office and the road

dipped down over a rattling timber bridge. The river rushed over rounded rocks on either side and then disappeared around a bend.

On the other side of the bridge was a small township of corrugated-iron houses. There was a white timber church with an orange tiled roof and four perfect square windows along one side. The small belfry reached into a crystal-blue sky. Next to the church was a tired-looking building that Jess guessed was the town hall.

'Welcome to Mathews' Flat,' said Luke, keeping the ute at a slow crawl. He hung an elbow out the window and cast scrutinising eyes over the various buildings, yards and street corners.

'This is where you were born,' said Jess with wonder. It was kind of impressive that the place bore his family's name, or a derivative of it anyway. A name that was on a map was pretty cool. She didn't know of any town called Fairley, that was for sure.

'My parents are both buried here,' he answered. 'There's a cemetery nearby, apparently.' He steered the car around a corner and continued slowly, still gazing about, drinking in every detail of the place.

They passed half a dozen more houses and continued out of town, heading west. Luke began checking his odometer and after a five-minute drive he pulled over at a rusty forty-four-gallon drum slung on four star pickets.

A small wrought-iron gate swung open behind it. Carved into a small timber plank of wood, barely readable, was the property's name:

MATTY'S CREEK

Luke's face was tight as he stared through the windscreen at what lay beyond. He cut the engine.

'This is it,' he said, almost to himself. 'This is it.'

7

THE ABANDONED PROPERTY was little more than a sheep paddock, cradled in the shadow of a huge mountain. The fences leaned every which way and a fibro shack, half swallowed by choko vines, looked as though it might fall down any minute. Grey kangaroos grazed peacefully between the house and the front fence. More lay resting under the wide verandah of the house. Beyond that, a creek carved a deep channel through a treeless field. The only sounds were of birds at the creek and the distant bawling of a calf.

Jess watched Luke. His eyes darted from one thing to another, searching for something that might stir a memory. She followed his gaze, over rainwater tanks, sheets of corrugated iron, coils of fencing wire, tubs, broken machinery.

He got out of the ute. Jess let him walk through the gate and across the yard before hopping out herself and following at a distance. The smells of eucalyptus and dry grass filled her nostrils.

'Look at all this crap,' Luke said, turning back to her. 'The place is a junkyard.'

Suddenly he gave a loud mocking laugh. He swore and sank his boot into a tangle of wire that lay strewn across the ground. He kicked over a crate full of empty beer bottles and the sound of their crashing seemed to suddenly fill him with contempt. He laid his boots into everything in his path. Sheets of tin, a stack of old tiles, an oil drum sent rolling, old grease glugging out of it.

Jess stopped the drum and righted it. 'Stop it, Luke.'

But her words went unheard. He picked up a plank of timber and hurled it against the side of a tin shed. Then he grabbed at anything, bricks, rocks, old bottles, and launched them at the shed, sending loud bangs resonating across the valley.

'Luke, stop it,' Jess said again. 'You're scaring me!'

Her words halted him abruptly. He drew a long breath and stared fiercely at the house. She saw him fight for control, mouth tight.

Jess stayed quiet.

'I don't remember that ugly house,' he said in a bitter voice as he began to walk towards it. 'Dad lived here by himself. Why didn't I live here with him?' He was ranting. 'Why wouldn't a man want his son to live with him? I don't get it. Look at all the broken fences. I could have helped him. I could have put new walls on that old shed, I could have propped up that old verandah, strained those corner posts . . .'

He looked at Jess, his eyes whirling. 'I feel *so* ripped off.'

He began to walk towards the house. 'When I turned eighteen this all became mine.' He stopped and put his hands on his hips. 'Bit late now. Why didn't he bring me back here when he was alive? Why'd he even leave it to me at all?'

Jess followed him as he marched to the front door of the house. The verandah sagged dangerously and she leapt back when Luke kicked the door with his boot. It burst open, taking half the architrave with it, and swung limply off one hinge.

'No need to wreck the joint,' mumbled Jess, waving a cloud of dust away from her face.

Ignoring her and the dust, Luke stooped and walked in. Jess followed tentatively. The place reeked of rat droppings. The hallway was dark and narrow and ended at a small kitchen. There were still old plates in the sink. Luke stood in the middle of the small room and looked about.

'I remember Mum in here,' he said in a voice that was achingly sad.

He turned back to the hallway and peered through a half-opened door. 'I remember a Christmas tree and a train set made out of timber. I had a train set.' He was talking mostly to himself, seemingly searching for something that would link him to the place and make solid a vision of a family and a home. He put his shoulder against the door and tried to push it open, but it was barricaded with piles of rubbish.

Luke swore suddenly and Jess saw the thick tail end of a snake slither under a pile of old chaff bags. She swore too and banged against the wall as she turned hastily towards the front door. A chunk of plaster the size of her elbow made a small thud as it fell into the wall cavity, and more critters rustled indignantly.

'No need to wreck the joint,' laughed Luke as he clambered out after her. Suddenly everything seemed hysterically funny. 'See the size of that black snake?'

'Only the tail end but that was enough for me. And there are rats!'

Luke stopped laughing. 'I want to go back in and have a proper look around, see if there's anything good in there.'

'You do that,' said Jess. 'I'm going to see if there's anywhere to put the horses.' Dodger and Legsy had been on the float for hours and she was eager to get them off. She was also feeling alienated from this new and unfamiliar

Luke. He was being weirdly erratic and for the first time ever she felt a need to be away from him.

'I want to have a look around the yard too,' he argued, heading towards what looked like a sheep pen.

The fences were low and blocked in with mesh wire but they were more or less intact and would do for the night. There was knee-high grass, too, which Dodger would appreciate.

'Wish I'd brought second rugs for them,' said Jess as she led the horses off the float. 'It's so much colder here than at home.' She was beginning to shiver a bit herself.

'They'll be right.' Luke pointed to the shaggy black silhouette of a horse on a nearby hill. Its head was up and it was staring intently at them. 'That one's got no rug and it's okay.'

'He's used to it,' said Jess. She led the horses to the creek and let them take long, gulping drinks before she closed the gate behind them in the sheep yard. 'You guys look after each other,' she said to the two geldings. Dodger immediately started pulling at the grass.

'We'd better get back to the hotel,' said Jess, wanting to leave. 'Mrs Arnold will be looking for us.'

Jess watched Luke still stalking about the yard, seeming disconnected, hearing only something deep inside himself. He stared across the hillside again, past the shaggy black horse. 'The cemetery's over the hill there,' he said in a distant voice. 'See all the headstones?'

'No.' Jess stared across the property but could only see trees. Then she saw just a few small white shapes between them. Gravestones. 'Yes. I see them.'

Luke started walking.

'Do you . . . do you want me to come?'

He shook his head and kept walking. She watched him find a crossing over the river and rock-hop across.

The black horse snorted curiously as Luke made his way up the hillside and stood, feet apart and hands by his side at the top, a silhouette against the fading sky. He was still, tall like a statue for a long moment before he started walking again, slowly, and disappeared down the other side.

Jess made her way back to the car. She was freezing. She rummaged around in the back of the ute, pulled an old blanket out of Luke's swag and shut herself inside the cabin.

It felt so good to lie down along the bench seat and close her eyes, but sleep evaded her. She lay huddled in the blanket, with country tunes murmuring on the radio, thinking of Luke beside his parents' graves.

It was nearly dark when the driver's side door opened and Luke got in. He sat, staring out the window across the hillside.

'Find them?'

He turned, ran a hand along her cheek and nodded, his face unreadable.

'Okay?' she whispered.

He didn't answer, but turned and looked back out the window. Jess took in the fading light, the old house, the soft hills meeting at the foot of the mountain. She imagined blue-eyed horses running wild up there. She thought of a small boy, peering out of the window into the night. He was still the same boy, she realised.

'We've really got to go, Luke,' she said eventually. 'Mrs Arnold will be ropeable.'

He nodded again and started the engine.

8

AS THEY ROLLED into town Jess saw a LandCruiser parked out the front of the pub. Leaning against the dented front panel stood Mrs Arnold, arms folded, mad black curly hair springing all over the place. She had one half-dead ugg boot crossed over the other and an annoyed look on her face.

'Uh, oh,' said Luke.

'Thought you two might turn up some time,' said Judy Arnold. She straightened up and marched towards the ute.

Jess groaned.

Mrs A unleashed a diatribe. 'What the hell are you two playing at?' she stormed. 'We were supposed to drive down together. I promised your parents I'd keep an eye on you! Why are you so late and where are the horses?'

Fang let out a low-pitched warning growl but she

wasn't deterred. *'Down, you mongrel!'* she snarled, loud enough to bring a couple of locals out of the pub to check what all the palaver was about. Filth whimpered. Fang looked confused.

'The horses are down the road,' said Luke, stepping out of the car. 'They're safe.'

'At your new property, are they?' asked Mrs Arnold, curiosity quickly replacing anger. 'What's it like?' she demanded.

'Messy.'

'Much land?'

'A bit.'

'House?'

'If you'd call it that.'

Jess got out of the car. Behind Mrs Arnold, in the cruiser, she saw Grace with her face hard up against the window, waving and pulling faces. Relieved to have some lighter company, she stifled a giggle.

Judy began marching towards the pub. 'Get outta the car, Grace. Bring my bags. You guys get a room key yet?'

'Doesn't look like the sort of place that *has* keys,' said Luke, trudging after her.

The old pub was a small brick building with large timber doors. It was painted cream like the two tin sheds behind it, one of which had *BUNKHOUSE* scrawled on a handwritten sign. It had four doors, each one scabbed from a different junk heap and none fitting properly. It didn't look cosy.

'This place is unreal,' Grace enthused loudly. 'I love it!'

Inside, a lively fire danced in the hearth and cast a golden warmth around the lounge. A lone stockman was resting his beer on the mantelpiece, above which hung a huge wood saw and what looked like a shark's jaw.

A small, friendly-faced woman stood behind the bar. She had short cropped hair and earrings that dangled onto her polo-neck jumper. 'There's only one bunkroom left,' she said. 'It's got four beds, and it's twenty bucks per person with a continental breakfast. Only one problem, I can't seem to find the key.' She began hunting under the counter.

Both Jess and Luke stifled a laugh.

'But don't worry, even if we have to put you up at home, we won't let you sleep out in the cold tonight,' said their hostess. She looked up. 'Dunno what I can do, it's just not anywhere!'

'Can't we break in somehow?' suggested Luke.

The woman looked thoughtful, then shrugged. 'We could try, I s'pose.' She came around the counter. 'This way,' she said, pushing the big old door open and stepping out into the cold.

They traipsed behind her until they all stood in front of the bunkhouse door, trying to rub some warmth into their arms.

'Smoke rings, look!' said Grace, making like a fish and puffing misty little rings into the air in front of her.

'Where'd you learn that?' snapped Mrs Arnold.

'Harry showed me,' said Grace, sounding delighted. She popped out a few more.

Mrs Arnold shifted about with her hands in her pockets. 'Can we get in or what?'

Their hostess looked at the deadlock and frowned. Luke reached out to the window and with one hand slid the sash up. Jess had never seen a window slide up so smooth and fast.

The woman looked pleased. 'Allow me,' she said, clambering in headfirst. 'Well, bugger me,' she called from inside. 'I found the key!' She appeared at the doorway with a big smile and a key dangling from one hand. 'You wouldn't believe it, though, the beds aren't made up. Can you give me half an hour? Have a drink on the house while you're waiting.'

Jess was glad to be back in the pub next to the fire. It was cosy and warm, which she was quite sure the bunkhouse would not be. The bar had begun to fill with people and the noise level had reached a merry rumble of laughter and storytelling. Mrs Arnold came back from the bar with a tray of drinks. 'Well, I'll only need one of these,' she said, lifting a schooner of port from the tray and beholding the size of it.

'Like port, do ya?' grinned the stockman by the fire.

'I do,' said Mrs Arnold in a low growl, 'and I hate ringers.'

The man chuckled, unabashed. Grace chortled.

'Three pink lemonades for you lot,' Mrs Arnold said, handing the tray to Luke. 'You'll have to stay in the pool room, no minors allowed in here.'

'Thanks,' said Luke in a flat voice. He didn't point out that he was in fact eighteen.

The pool room was also small with a fireplace, and through the door to the pub they could see and hear everything that went on anyway. A barmaid walked in with some old egg cartons, a few sticks and a log. 'That oughta get you started,' she said, dumping it into the wood basket and hurrying back to the bar.

They'd just burned through the egg cartons without so much as a lick of flame catching on the log when their hostess came bouncing back in. 'Room's ready!'

At the bar, Mrs Arnold ushered Luke in front of her. 'He'll get it, he's loaded.'

'No, I'm not,' Luke protested.

'Well, I don't have any money. This was your bloody holiday, remember. Consider it my chaperoning fee.'

Luke handed the woman his credit card. She read the name on the front, then looked up and eyed him with great curiosity. 'You from around here?'

'I was born here, eighteen years ago,' said Luke.

The woman looked like she'd seen a ghost. 'You Matty's boy?' she whispered.

She looked at the lone stockman and tilted her head, gesturing for him to come over. She handed him Luke's card. 'Look at the name on this.'

The man held it up and pulled a pair of specs out of his top pocket. He read it carefully, then frowned. He looked at Luke. 'You're Matilda Matheson's son.'

Luke nodded.

'Luker the puker,' said the stockman with amazement. 'Don't you be barfing all over me floors again.' He slammed an open hand across Luke's back, nearly fulfilling his own prophecy. Then he looked at Mrs Arnold with distaste. '*She* the mum you got?'

The woman came around from the counter. 'You're little Luke. They took you away.' She had her hands over her mouth and was looking Luke over, as though trying to find a trace of his mother. 'Matilda was my best friend. What are you doing here? Where have you been? Have you been okay?' She spoke in a rush.

Luke just looked stupefied. 'You're Kitty. Kitty and Steve.'

'You remember us!' Kitty laughed and gave him a hug. She wiped a finger along the rim of her eyes. 'Matty's boy. My Matty. I miss her every day.' Then she laughed. 'You've got her beautiful hair.'

'What about my father?' asked Luke. 'Did you know Ernest Matheson?'

'Yeah, we knew Ernest, though we never knew that was his real name till his funeral. Everyone around here just called him Jack. That's him there!'

Steve pointed to a black-and-white photo pinned to the wall behind the bar. A man in a singlet and an old bushie's hat was pouring a beer down the throat of a horse. There were others in the photo, laughing.

'That was taken before the accident,' said Steve. 'They were good times back then. Real good times.'

'That's Rambo,' said Kitty, pointing to the horse in the photo. 'He's still at Matty's Creek. He and Jack were best mates.'

'I think we saw him,' said Jess, looking at the photo. 'He was up on the hill.'

'Yeah, that'd be him. That's near where Jack's buried, in the cemetery up there, next to Matty. Rambo never leaves the hill paddock. He knows Jack's there.'

They spent the rest of the night sitting at a tall table next to a roaring fire, eating gravy-soaked chips and listening to Luke's history unfold.

'Your dad was driving the night your mum died, Luke. He was pissed. Tried to drive through the crossing while it was flooded. Always the hero, the larrikin,' said Steve as he finished downing another schooner. 'He never got over it. He was just a different person after that. Did some time in prison, that's when you got taken away, then he went back to that farmhouse and just kinda lived like a hermit.'

'You used to look after me,' said Luke to Kitty.

'You were only four when the trial came up and Jack went to jail.' She looked at Luke with tears in her eyes. 'They wouldn't let me keep you. I promised Matty I'd look after you.'

'The mongrels,' said Steve, 'they said we didn't fit the criteria to be foster carers. We were like bloody family. Your dad did four years. By the time he got out, he thought you'd be better off without him.'

'Were you?' asked Kitty, and Jess could feel the weight in her words.

Both Mrs Arnold and Grace watched Luke, waiting for the answer. His face was still but Jess could see that his mind was processing. Would he tell them about being shunted from one foster home to another, about being bashed, kicked out of school?

'Eventually,' Luke said, sparing them the full truth, 'I met a really good bloke called Harry. He taught me to break in horses. He was the best, a real father to me.'

Kitty smiled warmly.

'He was my uncle,' said Grace proudly.

'My brother,' said Mrs Arnold, shooting a gnarly look at Steve.

Then all of sudden everyone was getting emotional about Harry. They told stories about droving and camp-drafting, about the number of people who had ridden through town on the day of his funeral, Harry doing the full monty on the back of the bushfire brigade's truck. Judy told stories that neither Jess nor Luke had even heard before. Finally the stories came around to brumbies.

'Well, you've certainly got brumbies in your blood,' said Steve, raising his glass at Luke. 'Doesn't surprise me at all that you're involved with horses. Your old man used to disappear for weeks up in those mountains. He knew them all, didn't he, Kit?'

'Yep. He kept records of all the foals each year and always knew if one went missing or if it was injured.'

'That's why we're here,' said Mrs Arnold. 'Some bastards have been putting some rough-lookin' brumbies through the sales up north. All we know is that they're from the tablelands.'

'Doesn't surprise me,' said Steve. 'There's been all sorts of trouble up on the mountain lately.'

'Catching a brumby has always been an initiation thing with the young fellas around here,' said Kitty. 'Like a rite of passage. Some of those horses trace back to the Walers. These kids' ancestors were in the war, they rode those horses into battle. They see it as their right to be allowed to catch them.'

'Most just take a few photos and let them go,' said Steve. 'Or they might break them in, if they know what they're doing. They make top station horses.'

'We've got no problems with that,' said Judy. 'Harry used to do the same thing, catch one here or there and train it up. It's the idiots without a clue, the ones who dump them at the saleyards to be dogged with their legs half ripped off that we don't like.'

Then Jess told them about Sapphire and the golden palomino they had seen at the Brisbane saleyards. 'We have reports about other ones, too,' she said. 'They all have blue eyes.'

'It's all the blow-ins,' said Steve. 'They come down here and want to go brumby-running. It's just a sport to them. But they cause all sorts of trouble. Horses injured. Stock all stirred up, not to mention the damage to the bush.'

'The locals have always kept the brumbies in these

hills kinda quiet,' said Kitty. 'Not many people knew they existed. But word seems to have got out.'

'It's their colour,' said Mrs Arnold. 'The blue eyes and the golden pelt. They'd be quite a prize to catch, I imagine.'

'They're gonna wipe those horses out if they keep going,' said Luke. 'I'm going for a ride up there tomorrow. I want to see what's going on.'

'You wanna be careful,' warned Steve. 'About five different boundaries meet up there. It's a no-man's land, virtually lawless. There's all sorts of crazy people doing stupid things.'

Luke shot Jess a look.

'It's real,' Jess whispered with awe. 'A no-man's land. Where the boundaries meet . . .'

She wanted to go there, too.

9

AS THEY LEFT the warmth of the pub later that night, Grace looked crushed. 'I want to go up the mountain too but Mum wouldn't let me bring a horse.'

'Take old Rambo,' said Kitty, as she showed them to the bunkhouse again. 'He's old, but by geez he knows those mountains.'

Luke coughed.

Grace looked at him pleadingly. He shrugged. 'Okay.'

When they got to their room, it was freezing cold and no one had remembered to turn the tiny oil heater on. The beds were saggy and covered with purple chenille bedspreads with only one blanket. Kitty didn't seem to mind when Luke's two wolf-dogs slunk in after them.

'Cockroach spray. How thoughtful,' said Grace after Kitty had left. She picked up a blue can from a small timber dresser and gave it a shake.

'Here's the continental breakfast,' said Jess, opening a big plastic tub full of cups and plates and pulling out a snack pack of cornflakes.

'Any milk?' asked Mrs Arnold, peering over her shoulder.

'Can't see any.'

'Hmmm, crunchy.'

'I bags Fang for the night,' said Grace, whistling the big black dog up onto her bed. 'Lie down, boy!'

Luke appeared at the doorway with his swag.

'Where do you think you're going?' said Mrs Arnold, blocking the entrance.

'Out of the cold,' he answered, looking over her shoulder. 'It's arctic out here!'

'You got a whole house down the road – this is the girls' room!'

To Jess's horror, Mrs Arnold closed the door on him. Luke banged angrily on it. 'The house is full of black snakes and rats. Anyway, I paid for that room!'

'You've got a swag,' she called back, sounding unconcerned. 'Or are ya still *Little Lukey*?' She beat him to the window and flicked the catch across the top of the sash.

'*HEYYYY!*' he yelled.

'Keep your voice down. You'll wake the other guests.' Mrs Arnold flung the curtain shut and turned to the girls.

'Get changed and into bed. Big day tomorrow.'

'Can I at least have my dogs?' Luke called from outside.

'No, they'll freeze out there!' Mrs Arnold plonked her overnight bag on the bed that was under the window, effectively blocking any chance of him communicating with Jess. Filth leapt onto the fourth bed and nuzzled into the chenille bedspread gratefully.

'There you go, little doggy,' said Mrs Arnold, giving him a pat. 'You snuggle up there and stay warm.'

Jess curled into a heat-conserving ball and let the details of Luke's past churn around in her head. She wondered where he would sleep and hoped he wouldn't go back to the property. After listening for the engine of the ute to fire up for what seemed like hours, she finally relaxed and gave a low whistle. 'Filth,' she whispered softly.

The bed creaked and she felt it sag. The big shaggy dog settled down next to her and she gratefully wrapped her arms around his warmth. Finally her thoughts led her into sleep.

Jess rose as soon as she heard the first bird. She wrapped her jacket around herself, slipped her feet into her boots and quietly creaked the door open. Cold air rushed in but

Mrs Arnold kept snoring contentedly. Fang opened one eye and closed it again. All Jess could see of Grace was one arm flopped over the dog.

Outside, the sky was still dim with night and everything was shadowy. She stood next to Luke's ute and tried to stretch the saggy bed out of her spine. Her back complained bitterly while she spent a minute arching and bending and trying not to wake Mrs Arnold with her groaning. When she felt nearly vertical again, she looked around, wondering where Luke had spent the night.

Something cold wrapped around her ankle. A hand. Under the ute, she could see the edge of Luke's swag. 'I nearly died out here last night,' he said. He went on to call Mrs Arnold a string of unflattering names. 'I nearly freeze-branded my bum on that toilet.'

Jess crouched down. 'Open up.'

He lifted the cover of the swag and she crawled in next to him, boots and all. His freezing cold nose nuzzled into her neck and she giggled as he made her skin tingle. 'I was hoping you'd sneak out,' he said.

'I can't wait to go riding today,' she whispered.

'Me neither,' he whispered back. 'Can you believe what Steve said? About the no-man's land, all the boundaries meeting.'

'It's like your mum's stories,' whispered Jess. 'It must be a real place.'

'I couldn't stop thinking about it all night. My head nearly imploded. My parents are both buried here. I could hear the river where my mother died. I was haunted by them all night. It was *weird* sleeping here.'

'Good weird or bad weird?'

'Dunno,' he said. 'But I can't wait to go back to the property. I want to find the place in Mum's stories.'

'You weren't freaked out about the way . . . you know . . . your mum . . .'

Luke took a lingering breath. 'I hate alcohol,' he answered quietly. 'I'm never ever drinking.'

Mrs Arnold burst suddenly out of the bunkhouse door. She was a scary sight in her limp old nightie with hair poking out at strange angles. *'Jessica!'* she hissed, casting around the carpark. *'Jessica!'*

Jess felt the swag cover being shoved over her head. 'Shhh,' Luke laughed softly. She huddled in the warmth of his chest, where she could hear the beat of blood through his heart. He wrapped his arms protectively around her. 'Old cow stole my dogs, she's not getting my girl,' he whispered under the covers. He lifted his head again and let out a piercing whistle.

Mrs Arnold swore as Filth cannoned past her. She mumbled something about bloody teenagers. Just before she slammed the door shut, Fang escaped too.

After much sniffing and peeing, the dogs found Luke

under the ute and wagged apologetic tails at him. 'On the back,' he growled at them, pointing to the tray of his ute.

'Let them in,' Jess said, rubbing Filth's nose.

'No way! They've lost their swag privileges. Get on the back, you disloyal mutts!'

The dogs leapt onto the ute like water flowing back up a waterfall.

'Let's get going early,' said Jess, resurfacing. 'I want to check on Dodge.'

'Kiss me first,' said Luke, running his cold, work-cracked hands along her neck and up into her hair. 'Before the old hag busts you out here.' She snuggled into the warmth and rustle of the swag and felt herself almost drown in his arms and lips and gorgeous soft whisperings.

The idea of jumping back out into the frosty cold morning was left behind until Mrs Arnold, fully clothed and in steel-capped boots, kicked at the swag from the side of the ute. 'That's enough of that, you two, get up!'

'*Lukey Pukey's* making *me* wanna barf,' said Grace, walking past in pyjamas and boots with no socks, a towel over one arm and a wash bag under the other.

When Grace and Mrs Arnold were both in the bathroom, Luke grinned at her. 'Quick, let's nick off again!'

The property looked more inviting in the morning light. Kookaburras chortled in the gum trees and birds flitted down by the creek. The family of kangaroos grazed in a nearby paddock. A huge buck stood guardedly, staring unblinkingly at Jess and Luke until they were at a safe distance.

Luke picked up an old shovel and stepped through the front door of the house again. 'Look out, snakes,' he said as he disappeared.

Jess went to the sheep yard to check on Dodger and Legsy. She found them finishing the remains of last night's hay, with a thick coating of crunchy white frost across their backs. Mist billowed intermittently from their nostrils. Dodger seemed unperturbed, but Legsy chewed with a tight muzzle and his ears pinned back.

On the hillside behind them Jess noticed the shaggy black horse staring at them.

'Hello Rambo!' she called out. The horse flicked an ear back and forth, then walked away. One ear remained turned in her direction, she noticed.

Jess haltered Dodger and Legsy with red, icy hands and led them to the float so they could be saddled. Mrs Arnold's LandCruiser rumbled down the road towards them.

'I'm going to ride Rambo,' said Grace, leaping out of the car with a halter in her hand. 'Where is he?'

Jess pointed up onto the hillside. It was like sending a kelpie after a mob of sheep. Grace sprinted off.

A side window on the house burst open. 'Hey, Jessy! Come and look at this!' Luke held a bundle of maps and papers in his hands. 'I found Jack's records, look!'

Luke climbed out the window and spread his findings out over Legsy's horse rug. He unfolded a dog-eared topographic map, full of holes and splits at the creases. On the back was what looked like a big family tree, scrawled in different pens over many years.

'They're horse names,' said Luke excitedly. Next to each was a year, a gender and a colour. Many were noted as having one or two blue eyes. The chart seemed to skip generations and peter out here and there. Most of the names at the top of the tree were crossed out.

Jess and Mrs Arnold crowded around Luke.

The maps covered nearly forty years. According to Jack's last records, there were still at least six families of wild horses living up in the surrounding mountains.

'They go back to Saladin, like the Guy Fawkes horses,' said Mrs Arnold, pointing to a list of horses' names that were off to one side with question marks around them.

'"1999, *Beech Boy*. Creamy colt. Two blue eyes." I bet that's Sapphire,' said Jess, leaning over and placing her finger on some blue texta scrawl. She traced her finger along several lines to other names. 'He's sired others, and look down here, he had different mares during different years. There are no others with two blue eyes.'

'Here's one,' said Luke, stabbing at a name. 'Granite.'

'It's a bay,' said Jess.

They searched all over the brumbies' family tree and found no other horses with two blue eyes. About a third of them had one blue eye. Many were creamies or versions of creamies: palominos and buckskins, out of chestnuts and bays. There were a couple of golden colts with one blue eye and Jess wondered if one of them was the poor stretched animal they'd seen at the saleyards.

Luke flipped over to the topographic map and pointed to a spot. 'We can get up into the mountains from here.'

Jess looked up to see Grace walking down from the hill paddock with a halter on her shoulder and a frustrated look on her face. 'We've got Buckley's of catching that horse,' she said. 'Damn, I want to ride.'

Jess and Mrs Arnold went to help Grace while Luke continued poring over the maps and brumby records.

Out on the hillside, Rambo did not want to be caught. Jess noticed, however, that the horse's attention kept going past them, back to Luke.

'He keeps staring at you,' called Jess. She wondered whether Luke had the same form and shape as his father, or the same smell, the same voice and shaggy hair, perhaps.

Luke hopped over the fence and walked easily towards the horse.

Jess watched in amazement as Rambo allowed Luke to come close, standing still and quiet. 'Hey fella,' he said softly, running a hand under its heavily bearded jaw. He brushed the thick dreadlocks of forelock from the horse's forehead and revealed a startling sapphire blue eye.

'He's a brumby,' Luke whispered with quiet reverence. 'He's got the blue eye.'

Jess got goosebumps. 'He thinks you're Jack,' she whispered.

The horse nosed Luke gently, sniffed him all over and then put his head down near Luke's feet and kept it there.

'What are you doing?' Luke asked. He put an arm over the horse's thick, strong neck.

Rambo tossed his head up suddenly, sending Luke sprawling onto his backside. The horse looked shocked, and jumped back a couple of steps.

'Hey!' laughed Luke from the ground. 'What was that all about?' He pulled himself up onto his feet.

After some ear-waggling, Rambo walked back to him, put his head down at Luke's feet again and stayed there.

'That's an old bushie's trick,' said Mrs Arnold. 'He's trying to lift you onto his back!'

This time Luke put two arms over Rambo's neck and

once more the horse flung his head and neck upwards. Luke was ready for it this time, and he let Rambo lift him off the ground. He instinctively split his legs, threw one over the horse's back and sat upright. Rambo quivered through his shoulders but stood firm.

'Never got on a horse *that* way before!' Luke rubbed Rambo's shoulders. 'You're a bit of an old character, aren't you?'

Rambo turned around. With a swish of his tail he dismissed the girls and slowly plodded away from the house towards the mountain on his clumpy, split hooves and stiff old feathered legs.

'Jump on the horses and follow,' Luke called back to them. 'And grab the maps!'

10

THANKS TO RAMBO'S ambling pace, Jess and Grace were able to saddle the other horses, canter through the creek and easily catch up to the big black horse. Mrs Arnold followed at a distance in her old LandCruiser with Filth and Fang chained to the back seat lest they eat wild dog poison. Grace immediately started complaining that *she* had wanted to ride Rambo.

'He doesn't like you,' said Luke, his feet swinging nonchalantly back and forth by the horse's sides. 'He only likes me.'

Jess laughed at Luke's teasing and Grace shot her a cranky look. 'Don't expect me to double him home if the old nag conks out.'

They discovered there was no back fence to the property; farmed land just gradually turned into wilderness. Jess marvelled that Rambo stayed near the house by choice.

'Well, he *is* only a gelding,' said Grace, as though she'd lost interest in him. 'The wild stallions would probably beat the crap out of him.'

Luke ducked as Rambo carried him under the branch of a tree and began scrambling up a steep track. As the forest got thicker, the track became narrow and windy. Dodger and Legsy fell in behind Rambo. Mrs Arnold's fourbie roared and pitched and made scratching noises as it brushed through the dense shrubs.

Dodger blew heavily, pushing his shoulders into the climb. Jess gave him to the buckle of her reins and pulled her weight up and off his back. Drawing in mouthfuls of cold, thin air, she looked across wave after wave of tree-covered mountains, split by steep ravines and jagged cliffs. She wondered how anyone could find a brumby, let alone catch one, in that sort of terrain.

Rambo led them along an open ridge-top and then dropped back into a treed gully.

'I'll drive along the ridge-top and meet you on the other side,' called Mrs Arnold from the window of the fourbie. She was clearly frustrated that she couldn't follow them. 'If you don't find me, meet me back here on the ridge in an hour!'

Grace gave her the thumbs up and they continued on through the gum trees, tussocky snow grass and lichen-covered boulders.

As they rode, they discovered that the country was full of wombat holes. On every second rock was a neat deposit of square poo, and beneath every second log there was a burrow entry with a pile of soil beside it. A person would have to be nuts to gallop a horse through this country, thought Jess. It was tough going at a walk.

'Look! Snow clouds!' said Luke.

'How do you know they're *snow* clouds?' asked Grace.

Luke shrugged. 'I dunno, sounds good.'

Jess looked up. The clouds were thick and purple, unlike any she had seen before, and the air icy. She wondered if Luke was right, subconsciously drawing on some ingrained local wisdom about the weather.

They climbed another ridge and came out onto a four-wheel-drive track, where Mrs Arnold caught up with them. Two long wheel ruts cut through the open wooded hillside, with little sun orchids and slender rice flowers growing amid the grasses.

Jess felt a soft cold fluttering on her cheek, and then another. She looked around her. Was that ash blowing silently through the air? She couldn't smell smoke, and it was too cold for a fire.

Grace suddenly squealed. 'Oh my God, it's *snowing*!'

Jess caught her breath. She had never seen snow before. The tiny flakes stuck to her clothes and danced magically and weightlessly through the air and among the trees. They landed on her hair and tickled her nose and cheeks. She laughed out loud.

The magic continued until gusts of wind began to rustle the trees. Branches creaked overhead. Jess zipped her coat up around her throat and looked warily at the swaying tree limbs above.

Rambo raised his head and snorted. His pace slowed, then he stopped, and no amount of kicking or urging could make him move. Luke slipped off him and before he could grab the horse's mane, Rambo turned around and began walking, like a robot, into the wind, straight back to where he'd come from.

'Hey, don't just leave me here!' Luke called after him.

Grace snorted. 'Guess he doesn't like the cold. Told you he'd conk out.'

Then Legsy propped as well.

Mrs Arnold jumped out of the fourbie and cast her eyes about. 'Stallion droppings,' she said, pointing to a mound of horse poo. Snow whirled over it and settled on top. A short whinny sounded from behind them.

'Was that Rambo?' Jess spun around. It was hard to tell which direction it had come from, but she had the strong sensation she was being watched. Dodger trembled beneath her.

Somewhere, a branched snapped. There was a burst of galloping hooves, which abruptly stopped.

'I don't think Rambo could move that fast,' said Grace, gathering up her reins. Legsy began dancing beneath her.

'Don't let go of him,' said Luke, looking worriedly at Grace sitting on his good horse.

'I've got him,' she assured him.

'I think we might be in someone else's territory,' said Mrs Arnold. But she kept wading through the bush, negotiating logs and tangled thickets.

A horse whinnied again. More branches crashed. There was a drum of hoofbeats, and loud squeals.

'There's more than one!' said Grace, craning her neck around. She struggled to hold Legsy, who started rearing on the spot.

Then Mrs Arnold swore angrily. 'There! A mare, tied to that tree, look! Bait for the brumbies!'

She quickened her pace, leaping over a trickling creek and scrambling up an embankment.

Without warning, a great brown stallion exploded out of the bushes, causing branches to splinter and snap. He roared savagely and charged towards them.

Grace screamed. Legsy bolted. The stallion thundered after them with its ears back, teeth bared. Legsy carried a shrieking Grace out of Jess's sight. Suddenly the whole mountain was going crazy.

The stallion wheeled and galloped to the ridge-top. Meanwhile, Dodger began leaping out of Jess's hands in a way he had never done before. His shoulders trembled.

'Go back to the car!' yelled Mrs Arnold.

Jess let Dodger bolt after Legsy and found Grace next to the car, in tears. 'I thought it was going to kill me!' she cried. 'And I've lost Legsy!'

Jess dismounted. Next second, Dodger too broke away, tearing the reins from her hands and disappearing down the same track as Rambo. She was shocked but tried to stay upbeat.

'As long as they don't go near that mare, they should be okay,' she puffed, listening to Dodger's hoofbeats fade. 'They should just follow Rambo back to Matty's Creek.' She hoped she sounded more confident than she felt. This was an enormous wilderness to lose a horse in. 'Where's Luke?'

Grace pointed to the high branches of a snow gum. Luke clung precariously to an upper limb. 'He's safe.'

The girls climbed onto the bonnet of the LandCruiser. Jess felt the metal clunk and buckle under her boots. On the opposite hillside, a lean white mare struggled against a hemp rope tied around her neck. She gave a frightened whinny. Three colts circled her.

'They're all fighting over her,' said Grace. 'Poor thing, she's terrified.'

The brown stallion, his pelt covered in battle scars, charged at the colts. He was lathered with froth and sweat, and roaring with fury. But while he hunted one colt away, the others circled closer to the mare.

The stallion returned and chased the other two until finally they retreated.

'They're still watching from the hilltop,' said Grace. She pointed. 'Look!'

The two colts, one bay, one creamy, paced back and forth along the ridge, tails swishing, never taking their eyes off the mare.

'This could go on for days,' said Jess.

The stallion nudged and pushed at the mare, trying to move her, to claim her as his and take her with him, but the rope held her fixed to the tree. The stallion bit at her. He swung his hindquarters and kicked at her with frustration. She gave a pleading squeal.

Fang started growling in the back of the car, then barked loudly. He was a scary sight at full throttle, with huge black jaws and slobber flying everywhere.

'There are wild dogs circling her too!' said Mrs Arnold, joining them at the car. She pointed to a dark shadow slinking under a log. 'We've got to untie that mare!'

She stepped up onto the running boards and looked into the treetops. 'I've got a good knife in the glovebox. Luke'll have to cut the rope.'

'Cut the rope, are you kidding?' said Jess. 'The stallion will kill him.'

Mrs Arnold ignored her and dived into the front of the car. In moments she resurfaced with the knife. Jess watched as she ran to the tree where Luke was perched.

She couldn't hear the conversation, but she saw Luke clutch the tree limb even tighter. He stared down at Mrs Arnold as though she was nuts. Mrs Arnold thrust the knife towards him.

After frantic gesticulating, she came storming back to the car. '*Baby Lukey* wants us to let his dogs out.' She wrenched open the back door of the car.

Filth and Fang threw themselves gleefully into the chaos. They bounded after the bachelor colts, whirling around bends and flying over boulders and logs, howling as they went. The colts scattered into the bush.

Luke slipped out of the tree and scrambled across the hillside. He clambered over rocks and ducked under half-fallen trees. He reached the mare and lunged at the rope.

'Go, Luke!' whispered Jess as she watched him hack at it.

'Look out, the stallion!' Mrs Arnold suddenly screamed. She climbed onto the bonnet of the car and it warped under her weight.

Luke looked up. The stallion bore down on him, teeth bared.

Jess, Grace and Mrs Arnold all jumped up and down, pointing and yelling.

Luke dropped the knife and ran, leaving the mare still tethered.

Fang flew out of nowhere and, with an impressive rush of snarls and woofery, threw himself at the nose of the stallion. It roared in fury and struck out with its front hooves.

Luke dived for shelter under a large fallen tree.

The stallion shook off the dog and charged after Luke. Jess watched aghast while Luke curled into a tiny ball against the trunk and shielded himself against the stallion's striking hooves.

Fang launched at the stallion's back legs, snarling savagely. Filth joined him. The noise was horrendous. The stallion spun on them and with his head low, ears pinned, he hunted them back across the hillside.

'Run, Luke!' Jess screamed. 'Run now!'

Luke shot out from under the tree and bolted, tripping and rolling and leaping until he reached the car, climbed in and slammed the door shut behind him. He lay on the back seat, gasping for air.

Jess ripped open the opposite door and found him clutching at his arm. 'I thought that thing was going to kill you!' she said.

Luke screwed up his face and looked at the ceiling. 'I think I broke my wrist again,' he groaned.

'Look, look!' yelled Grace excitedly, stomping more

dents into the bonnet. She pointed to the mare. It had broken the last shreds of the half-cut rope and was galloping off into the forest, the brown stallion cantering after her. 'She's free!'

'You did it, Luke!' said Jess.

'Now that's not a bad retirement plan for an old girl,' said Mrs Arnold, smiling as she watched them disappear over the ridge-top.

11

LUKE FINALLY AGREED to let Mrs Arnold look at his wrist. 'Doesn't look broken to me,' she said, giving it a squeeze. He shrieked and pulled away.

'Well, maybe a little hairline fracture,' she conceded. She found two straight sticks and ripped half an old shirt into bandages, then used the other half to make a sling.

Luke snatched it from her with his other hand. 'I'll do it myself,' he grumbled. 'I don't want you going anywhere near it.' He began using his teeth and his good arm to wrap his wrist. 'Some chaperone you are.'

'Need some help?' asked Jess.

He handed her the torn rags. 'Thanks.'

Jess gently strapped his wrist and slung it snugly against his chest. There was no obvious bump or swelling but she could see the veins in his forearm pulsating strongly as she helped put his jacket back over his shoulders.

'I'm going to call the dogs back,' Luke said, putting two fingers between his teeth and giving an ear-splitting whistle.

As he set off to find his dogs, Jess turned to the others. 'Why would someone tie up that mare?' she asked.

'Like I said, to lure the stallions,' said Mrs Arnold. 'They let them fight over the mares for days until they're exhausted. Then the runners come back and try to catch them.'

'Don't they realise how cruel that is?' said Jess.

Mrs Arnold snorted. 'It's just a sport to them. They don't care about the horses. Half the time they just go back home and forget about them. They do the same with their traps. They come back months later, when it suits them, and find a pile of carcasses in there.'

'Was she a wild mare, do you think?'

'Nah, she had brands. They probably just picked her up from the knackery.' She cast her eyes over the surrounding hills. 'They'll have traps set around here for sure.'

'Let's look for them,' said Jess, 'and pull them apart.'

'Okay,' Mrs Arnold said. 'But they'll be well hidden.' She climbed into the car and pulled Jack's maps out of the glovebox. 'Maybe the old fella will give us some clues.'

She carefully unfolded the topographic map over the steering wheel and ran her finger over Jack's little Xs and marks. 'If I were going to trap brumbies, where would I put yards?' she mumbled to herself.

'Near their water,' said Grace, poking her head in the window.

'Where you could get a truck in,' added Jess.

'Somewhere not far from where they tied the mare . . . We'll have to go out on foot,' said Mrs Arnold, closing the map. 'Wish we still had horses.'

'So do I,' said Jess, with gnawing apprehension. 'I hope they went back to Matty's Creek.'

Mrs Arnold gave her a reassuring wink. 'I can't imagine old Dodger wanting to join the wild bush horses,' she said. 'Or Legsy. They both like two good feeds a day and a warm rug. They'll be okay. They'll follow the old one down.'

Jess hoped she was right. She found an old jumper in the back of the fourbie and wrapped it around her head and neck to keep warm, then set off for the ridge-top with icy mist blowing from her lungs and snow sticking to her clothes like little barbed icicles.

The snowflakes grew thicker as she walked, and they began to stick to the gum leaves and grasses. At the ridge-top Jess looked out across a whirling white blizzard. She could no longer see the layers of distant mountains. She and Grace trailed Mrs Arnold along a narrow brumby track across the ridge-top and through sparser eucalypt forest.

'Tyre marks,' Grace suddenly yelled. 'A truck has been through here!'

They followed the ground-up muddy tracks through a trickling stream, around rocks, past deep ruts and disturbed ground where a vehicle might have been bogged. At the top of another hill Mrs Arnold abruptly stopped and put her hands on her hips.

'There! Knew it wouldn't be too far away.'

In a small, flat hollow was a set of heavy steel cattle yards, built out of panels and linked together with metal pins. They were the portable kind that could be easily dismantled and thrown on the back of a truck. They'd been set up as a funnel-shaped laneway, leading into a square yard.

'Trap yards,' said Grace.

'No, they're not,' said Mrs Arnold, as she approached them. 'There's no salt and no lucerne. No one-way gate, and no water. These are holding yards.'

They kept searching and found a four-wheel-drive ute with a large livestock crate on the back, thinly camouflaged under a few broken gum-tree branches. The numberplates were missing and the back window was smashed in. Attached to the crate was a heavy-duty winch, the kind used to drag large boats onto trailers. Jess felt her stomach churn as images of struggling brumbies shot through her mind. She looked at the large snap hook, dangling from the wound-up chain. So it was true. They really did use boat winches to load them.

She thought of Sapphire's mares and the little buckskin foal back at Harry's place, with their scarred faces and bruised souls. She imagined Sapphire, chained to the side of this truck, being hauled by the head and tail through this rough country, fighting all the way. All the romance of wild bush horses and bearded stockmen *gathered to the fray* suddenly made her feel sick. This was the reality of brumby-running, staring her in the face. She had already seen where the wretched creatures ended up.

Mrs Arnold pulled open the door of the vehicle and pointed to wires dangling from the ignition. 'It's been hot-wired,' she said. 'Wonder if it's stolen.' In the passenger footwell they found food wrappers, empty cigarette packets and beer bottles. 'Teenagers,' she grunted with disapproval. There was more rubbish scattered on the ground outside the car, and tyre marks all through the dirt. It looked like other vehicles had been there, too.

Mrs Arnold pulled out her phone and began taking photos of the car and yards and the damage to the forest. She reached into the driver's side and pulled the bonnet release, taking photos of the engine and chassis numbers. 'For the cops,' she said to Jess.

'Let's pull the yards apart! That'll stop them,' said Grace.

'No, they'll just put them back together again,' said Mrs Arnold. 'We need to do more than that. Start pulling out the pins and put them in your pockets. We'll take them with us.'

Jess and Grace began work on the yards, pulling the pins from top and bottom and letting each panel fall to the ground with a clang.

When all the panels lay in a heap, Mrs Arnold climbed inside the runners' car. 'Let's see if the old girl goes,' she said, fumbling with the wires and giving it a kick in the guts. It spluttered and gave a few false starts, then coughed to life with a billow of black smoke behind it.

'Get out of the way!' she yelled, as the last few panels fell to the ground. She crunched the car into gear and pointed it straight at them.

Jess and Grace leapt out of the way and then cheered with delight as Mrs Arnold ploughed over the pile of steel, then roared the ute back and forth, grinding the gears and revving the engine. The panels buckled and bent under the weight of the car until they lay in a mangled heap. After a final defiant roar and blurt of smoke, Mrs Arnold killed the engine and stepped out with a satisfied gleam in her eye.

'Woo hoo! Madam Demolition strikes again,' whooped Grace, punching the air.

Jess was doubled over with laughter. She looked over her shoulder. 'I hope those runners don't come checking their traps any time soon.'

'Wasn't us,' said Mrs Arnold, slamming the car door shut and climbing down off the mountain of tangled steel. 'We just found it like this, didn't we, girls?'

'Yep,' said Jess, still chuckling.

'We better skedaddle, just in case,' Mrs Arnold grinned. 'One more thing.' She opened the bonnet of the car, reached in, fumbled about and resurfaced with two small pieces of wire in her hand. 'Let's take these too,' she said, handing them to Grace. She set off into the forest, leaving the car with its bonnet gaping open.

'Wonder how Luke went with the dogs,' said Jess, skipping behind her.

They headed back to the LandCruiser full of triumph and satisfaction, their pockets heavy with metal pins.

'That was about five grand's worth of yard panels,' said Grace, bouncing over a log. 'I know, 'cause Dad just bought some at the start of the year, and that's how much they cost.'

'Another reason I want all the pins,' said Mrs Arnold slyly. 'I'm going back for the gates, too. Reckon I could get them on my roof racks?' She looked sideways at Jess. 'My demolition fee.'

'You slippery old woman,' chuckled Grace.

Jess hurried to the ridge-top, keen to see Luke and the dogs again. From the top, through the whirling snow and the gusts of wind, she could see Luke crouching, his shoulders slumped. Something wasn't right.

12

LUKE WAS SITTING in a patch of grass and ferns nursing Filth's big head, sobbing unashamedly. Fang sat silent beside him.

'Oh, Luke,' she whispered.

'Oh God, Jess, he's dead. He's dead.' Tears were pouring down his face. 'Wake up, fella,' he cried, stroking Filth's ears and running his hand over the dog's shaggy chest. 'Come on, boy, wake up!'

Jess turned and motioned for the others to stop.

'Oh *crap*,' she heard Mrs Arnold say.

'He saved me,' sobbed Luke. 'He doesn't deserve to die.' He looked at Jess with red-rimmed eyes. 'Why does everyone have to die? I can't handle it!'

'Luke . . .' Jess didn't know what to say. She was so shocked. 'One of the brumbies must have kicked him.'

'Are you sure he's dead?' asked Mrs Arnold, stepping closer.

Something warm and rancid seeped through the air, and Jess could have sworn she saw Filth's tail lift slightly.

'He sure smells like it,' mumbled Grace quietly.

Jess looked daggers at her. Grace shrugged, covered her nose with one hand and took a few steps back.

'He just whined,' said Mrs Arnold, stepping closer to the dog and crouching down. She ran her hand over Filth's head. 'Stop your bloody wailing, Luke,' she said. 'I can't hear him.'

Luke stopped sobbing. Between his sniffs Jess could hear, faint but unmistakable, a low whine.

'Oh God, he's still alive.' Luke began sobbing even louder. 'He's not dead. He's alive. What do I do?' He seemed in a panic. Fang got up and began nuzzling him around the face.

'Shut the hell up, for a start. Crikey, what's wrong with you?' snapped Mrs Arnold. 'Let me look at him.' She ran her hands carefully over the yellow dog's body, pressing and poking here and there.

'I think he's been kicked in the neck,' she finally said. 'Or the head. Maybe both.'

'He needs a vet,' said Grace. 'We have to get him back down the mountain somehow.'

'How will we get him to the car?' said Jess. She reckoned Filth must weigh more than she did, and with his injuries it wasn't going to be easy to move him.

'There's an old bedspread in the back of the fourbie,' said Mrs Arnold. 'Run and grab it, Gracie. We'll use it as a stretcher. Between the four of us, we should be able to carry him.'

'A *bedspread*?' said Grace. 'Why do you have a *bedspread* in your car?'

'Just go and get it, Grace!' said an exasperated Mrs Arnold.

While Grace did as she was told, Luke gently eased himself out from under Filth and knelt by the dog's head. 'Hang in there, Filthy,' he said softly to him. 'We'll get you back home, just hang in there, don't go dying on me.' He pulled his jacket off and draped it over Filth's chest.

Grace returned moments later with a bundle of purple chenille under her arm. 'Liked the decor just a bit too much, did we, Mum?' The bedspread was from the bunk-house.

Mrs Arnold shot her a defensive frown. 'In case we got cold. I was gonna give it back.'

'Yeah, right,' said Grace, handing the felonious item to her mother and helping her spread it out.

Filth weighed a tonne and he didn't seem able to move much, apart from the occasional shuffle of his legs, which brought whimpers and whines of pain. They stuffed the bedspread under him and dragged him onto it, then took a corner each and began hauling him across the wooded hillside. It was hard, awkward work, especially with Luke complaining about his arm. Fang trotted anxiously around them, sniffing and whining.

Lying down, the big yellow dog barely fitted in the back of the fourbie, and they had to move all manner of junk to the front seat, then leave the tailgate open with his back paws hanging out. Luke sat at his head. Jess and Grace dangled their legs from the back tailgate as Mrs Arnold drove slowly over the rutted tracks through the forest. They emptied their pockets of the heavy metal pins and tossed them in the back.

Fang followed the LandCruiser, sniffing at wombat poo and bolting after the occasional wallaby. They'd been going for less than half an hour when he suddenly rushed to the front of the car and began barking aggressively.

'Oh *crap*,' said Mrs Arnold, for the second time that day.

Another vehicle was approaching, a big blue F250 truck, groaning and revving as it pitched and rolled over the ruts in the track. On the back, inside a large cage, two enormous caramel-coloured dogs barked and snarled, slobber dripping from their jowls.

'Girls, get in the back seat, now!' ordered Mrs Arnold. 'Luke! Get that dog under control before he gets himself in a fight.'

Grace and Jess immediately scrambled over the seat and into the back. Luke got out and roared at Fang, who reluctantly trotted back to the fourbie, still growling and threatening over his shoulder. Luke reached down, slung a rope around his neck and used his one good hand to tie him somewhat awkwardly to the towbar.

The other car pulled up beside them and the driver rolled down his window. He was a middle-aged man, wearing a beanie and a checked jacket with a fur-lined collar. In the passenger's seat, another man slugged on a can of beer, then crushed the empty and tossed it out the window.

Mrs Arnold nodded a greeting. 'Boys.'

The driver nodded back without smiling. 'Nice day for it.' He ran scrutinising eyes over the fourbie.

'Yeah, not bad.'

'See any horses?'

'Yeah, a few,' said Mrs Arnold, not giving much away. 'They were pretty restless though, dunno why.'

'Yeah?' The man turned to his mate in the front. 'Sounds like it's gonna be a good weekend, Johnno.' They sniggered.

Mrs Arnold changed the subject. 'Good-lookin' dogs you got on the back there. Bull Arabs, are they?' The dogs were nearly as big as Luke's, but short-haired, with huge blocky heads and large limbs. They looked as though they were bred to bring down a horse, rather than just chase it. They held their noses high and whined into the wind.

'Yeah,' drawled the man, sounding pleased that she recognised them. 'They're on a scent now. There are horses close, I reckon.' He turned his head and scanned the countryside.

'Sight any yet?' asked Mrs Arnold.

'Dogs picked up a scent back further. We found tracks but the horses were shod. Must be weekenders riding up here.' Again he ran his eyes over Mrs Arnold, the fourbie, Fang tied to the towbar as Luke held him steady with one hand, the other strapped to his chest.

The guy in the passenger seat let forth some profanities about do-goodie tourists and cracked another can.

'Painful, aren't they,' agreed Mrs Arnold.

Jess listened to her lying through her teeth, passing herself off as another brumby-runner. She shuddered as she thought of those dogs chasing Dodger. If only Mrs Arnold would stop fraternising with these freaks and take them back to the house so they could check that the horses were safe.

Mrs Arnold must have heard her thoughts. 'Yeah, well, we better be off,' she said. 'Bastard stallion kicked one of our dogs in the neck, gotta get it to the vet.'

This comment drew their interest. 'What did it look like?' asked the driver.

'White,' Mrs Arnold lied. 'With two blue eyes. Looked like a ghost horse or something. I wish we hadda caught it.'

'Never seen a white one up here,' said the driver, with a doubtful snort. 'A few creamies, but never a white.' He looked at his mate. 'You ever see a white horse up here, Jonesy?'

The other man shook his head. 'Nup. Caught a pale creamy one a few weeks back, and a couple of his mares. Wouldn't mind catching a white one, though. Where'd you see it?'

'On another trail,' said Mrs Arnold.

'And which trail would that be?' asked the driver with a challenging stare.

'Down by . . .' Jess caught her desperately searching for a name on the map that lay folded on the dash, '. . . Creeping Gully.'

'That's miles from here,' he answered, sounding suspicious.

'Yeah, well, we can't give too much away, can we?' said Mrs Arnold in a cool voice. She gave him a wink. 'We might wanna run that one ourselves.'

The man sneered. His passenger got out of his car and to Jess's horror began walking to the back of the fourbie. 'Give us a look at your dog.'

Fang let out a low growl and bared his teeth. The hair

down his back stood on end. Luke struggled to hold him with his one good hand.

'Good dog,' said the man, shifting his gaze to Fang and then to Luke. Then he looked past both of them, trying to see Filth in the back of the fourbie.

'Oh no, the yard pins,' Grace hissed at Jess.

But the man only gave Filth a quick glance. 'May as well shoot him. He's not gonna hunt again.'

'That one was a bit brain-damaged anyway,' said Mrs Arnold.

Luke shot an incensed look at her.

'I got a shotty in the back if you wanna borrow it.' The man nodded at Fang. 'That one's the better of the two anyway. Nice dog, that. What breed is it?'

'Mount Isa Runner,' said Luke. 'New breed, from up north. They're handy on cold scents, go all day, find the ones that are good at hiding.'

'Oh yeah?' said the man with a cynical smirk. 'He might help you get that white stallion. Though I don't know if he'll have the jaws to hold him once he finds him.'

'They'd have to run it down first,' said Luke, nodding at the other man's heavy-set dogs. 'And these guys come into their own when they're running. Good stamina and pace.' He gave Fang a blokey slap.

'Hard to find a dog that can do it all,' agreed the man.

He didn't take his eyes off Fang, Jess noticed. Then she had an idea.

'We got some of his pups at home, if you wanna buy one,' she said, poking her head out the window. The man looked startled, as though he hadn't noticed her there.

Luke looked just as startled, but had the presence of mind not to show his surprise.

'Petunia's pups!' said Jess. Petunia was Shara's pre-historic dog. She was a foxy cross and had been spayed for years.

'Oh yeah, *Petunia*,' said Luke, recovering well. 'Good bitch. Bit smaller than these guys, but real hard. Quick, too.'

'Might be interested in one of those pups,' said the man. 'Where did you say they were bred?'

'Mount Isa,' said Luke. 'Big country up there. Lots of brumbies, pigs, rogue cattle . . .'

'Feral dogs . . .' Grace added under her breath, and Jess jabbed her in the ribs with an elbow.

'They don't muck around with their dogs up there,' Jess piped in.

'Nah,' agreed the man. 'Mount Isa Runners, ay? Never heard of them.' He looked genuinely confused.

'They're hard to come by. Worth a fortune. Could put some stamina into your bloodlines,' said Luke.

'Give us your contact details and we'll let you know when they're ready to sell,' said Jess.

'Listen, we better head off,' said Mrs Arnold, sounding unimpressed. 'That snow is coming down heavier, be getting dark soon.'

The men scrambled around in their glovebox and scrawled some details on a scrap of paper while Jess tried to memorise their numberplate.

As he handed the paper to Luke, the man looked at Filth, still motionless in the back of the fourbie. 'Sure you don't wanna borrow that gun?'

'Nah, he's my old man's dog. We'll finish him off when we get him home, bury him in the backyard with the others.'

'Must've been a good dog, was he?'

'The best,' said Luke. It was the first truthful thing he'd said.

Mrs Arnold started the engine and began driving away. 'We better get out of here, *quick*,' she muttered as she hit the accelerator. 'Before those guys use that shotty on *us*!'

Jess felt the seat pull behind her and Luke's face appeared from the back of the car. 'You're a genius, Jessy,' he smiled, and planted a kiss on her cheek.

They travelled in anxious silence, knowing that, quite literally, they weren't out of the woods yet, as they searched desperately for the track that led back to Matty's Creek. As the snow spread a thick white blanket over the land, everything began to look the same.

Filth lay miserably in the back of the fourbie and Luke urged Mrs Arnold, 'We gotta get him to a vet. Drive faster; he's not going to last long.' Less than a minute later he was begging her to slow down. 'You're bumping around too much. It's hurting him! It's hurting *me*!'

'Make up your mind,' said Mrs Arnold, exasperated.

Finally, near dusk, she pointed through the windscreen. 'Look!'

Rambo stood on a ridge-top, the wind ruffling his mane and his nose to the breeze, watching them intently with his mismatched eyes.

'He's come to check on us,' said Mrs Arnold. 'I reckon he's taken the other horses home for sure.'

Jess looked out the window, allowing the snow to land lightly on her face and catch on her eyelashes. The slopes were thick with it now and Jess hoped like crazy it would be enough to cover the fourbie's tyre tracks before the brumby-runners found their mangled yards.

13

IT WAS WELL AFTER sunset when Mrs Arnold's battle-scarred LandCruiser bumped its way out of the forest and down the hill paddock. The snow had turned to rain now, and there were people in hats and oilskins walking around the property, lit by the headlights of several vehicles. Jess was enormously relieved to see the silhouettes of two saddled horses in the sweeping beams of light. She instantly recognised Dodger's nuggety silhouette.

'These guys came galloping through town with no riders,' said Kitty, as Jess jumped from the car and threw her arms around her horse's neck. 'We didn't know what had happened to you.'

'Everyone okay?' asked Steve, who was holding Legsy by a set of broken reins.

'We got attacked by a brumby stallion,' said Grace, leaning from the car window and launching into a full and enthusiastic account of the day. 'Shoulda seen it. I thought it was gonna *kill* Luke!'

'It kicked my dog,' said Luke from the back of the fourbie, where he had Filth's head cradled in his arms. 'He needs a vet.'

People Jess had never seen before began crowding around the back of the vehicle. 'What happened? What's wrong with him?'

'A brumby kicked him,' said Grace. 'There was a mob of bachelor colts and he was chasing them.'

'Who are all these people?' asked Luke.

'Just a few neighbours,' said Steve. 'When a fourth-generation local comes home, word spreads fast. When his horse comes galloping through town without him, they form search parties.'

'Let Barker have a look at him,' someone said, and the swarm of people parted like the Red Sea. A silver-haired man in a police uniform was pushed to the front of the crowd. 'Thirty-five years on the dog squad!' said another voice. 'He'll know what to do with him.'

Barker had a kind and craggy face with three days of stubble on his chin. He held a hand out to Fang, who sat next to Luke. Fang sniffed it and allowed the man to pat him. Then Barker ran gentle hands over Filth's slack body. 'What's he, a dingo?'

'Err,' Luke stammered.

'You know it's illegal to keep dingo hybrids in New South Wales.'

'Well, he's actually a Mount Isa Sniffer,' began Luke. 'They're a new breed from up north. Great on cold scents. He helped us find a big white stallion today.' Jess caught Grace and Mrs Arnold rolling their eyes at each other.

'But yeah, people often say they look a bit like dingos,' he continued. 'Must be the Asian bloodlines they mixed in, from Burma mostly. Big jungles up there, lots of exotic prey like lions and elephants and stuff.'

'Never knew there were lions in Burma,' said Barker, as he felt along Filth's spine.

'Oh yeah, there's heaps of them these days,' said Luke, 'especially since all this global warming and stuff. Yep! These dogs are pretty special, hard to come by. Surprised the dog squad up in the Isa aren't onto them yet.'

Barker and Steve exchanged cynical glances.

'Did we mention Luke was kicked by a brumby as well?' said Mrs Arnold. 'It got him in the head.'

'There'll be a litter of pups back home if you're interested,' added Grace.

Mrs Arnold changed the subject. 'There's a lot of illegal brumby-running happening up in those mountains,' she said. 'I've got plenty of evidence if you're interested in something factual.'

'That'd be good,' said Barker. He kept his attention on Filth. 'He can still move his limbs. Might just be bad bruising, but I reckon we'd better get him to a vet for some X-rays.'

'I s'pose I'll meet you at the police station in the morning,' said Mrs Arnold.

'We don't really have one of those around here,' said Barker. 'I usually just meet people at the pub.'

'Hence the lawless frontier,' said Mrs Arnold under her breath. 'The pub it is, then.'

Mrs Arnold helped them transfer Filth into the police wagon, using the controversial purple bedspread. 'Just distract that lady from the hotel for a minute,' she muttered to Jess.

'Yeah, it's a Mount Isa Shepherd,' Jess overheard someone else say. 'Poor thing was probably trying to protect some sheep. Be a shame to lose him. They're quite rare, apparently.'

With Filth loaded, Luke put an arm around Jess's waist and smiled. 'We got those brumby-runners good.'

'We did,' she grinned.

'You go back to the pub and get warm,' he said, giving her a squeeze. 'I gotta take my Mount Isa Runner to the vet.'

'Sniffer,' she corrected him. 'Or Mount Isa Shepherd, if you run into the postmaster.'

He chuckled. She shook her head.

'Reckon he could X-ray that arm for you while he's at it?'

'Maybe.' He gave her a kiss on the forehead and she suddenly realised how cold and exhausted she was. She squeezed him back, wishing he could come and snuggle up with her in front of that huge fire at the pub. 'I'll rub down Dodger and Legsy, make sure they're all right.' She waved goodbye and turned back to the horses. 'Come on, Grace.'

14

'STATE OF ORIGIN'S on tonight,' said Steve loudly. 'The Blues are gonna whip your Queenslander butts!'

The pub was busy, with men standing shoulder-to-shoulder, beers in hand, as they watched the state-of-origin match on TV. Grace and Jess were once again ushered to the pool room, where an empty wood basket stood next to a cold hearth.

'Let's go outside and look for some firewood,' said Grace. 'We'll freeze in here without a fire.'

They stepped out into the chilly night. A huge fig tree blocked out the moon, casting darkness all around them. Walking hand-over-hand along a smooth branch, a possum peered down at them with round, golden eyes like dollar coins. Jess patted her empty pockets. 'Sorry, little fella.'

She pulled her collar up around her ears and shoved her hands into the warm depths of her jacket. 'There are some gum trees out the back. Let's look there.'

Under the trees in the next paddock, the ground was thick with wet kindling and Jess began collecting twigs, snapping them against her knee and stacking them in piles. In the pub, voices rose and fell with the mood of the football. Glasses clinked, and every so often a burst of laughter erupted.

The noise increased whenever the front doors were opened. Mrs Arnold's voice rose over a chorus of footy fans. *'GO, YOU GOOD THING!'*

As the girls bundled up their firewood, a set of headlights swept over the paddock and Jess heard a truck rumble into the carpark.

'Ohhh,' Grace breathed quietly. She dropped her bundle of sticks. 'That's the brumby-runners' truck!'

The truck rolled to a standstill by the carpark and the driver wound his window down. It was them all right. The truck had a big crate on the back and there was a horse inside it, struggling to keep its feet.

'It's a brumby,' said Grace. She groaned. 'Ohhh, the *poor thing*!'

Inside the mesh cage, the horse screamed with the high, nervous pitch of a foal. 'It's a baby,' said Jess.

The truck didn't stop, but rolled on very slowly. Jess realised the drivers were casing the carpark. She crouched down in the long grass.

'I don't think they've come to watch the footy, some-how,' said Grace in a low, worried tone.

'They might be looking for us,' whispered Jess. 'And your mum's in the pub.'

There was a sudden explosion of barking. A torch snapped on and the light panned across the paddock. Grace cursed and threw herself to the ground.

Jess did the same and silently prayed the runners didn't let their dogs off. Those things were bred to pull down and kill horses. She couldn't imagine them having any trouble with a pair of scrawny teenagers. She looked at the flooded gum above her, searching for handholds, should she need them. A beam of light passed directly over her head.

Some nearby sheep bleated and she could hear their tiny hooves galloping towards the river. Next to her Grace was so quiet, Jess wondered if she was still there.

'Just sheep,' said a gruff voice. The torch snapped off and the same voice growled at the dogs. *'Max! Brutus! Siddown and shuddup!'*

Jess lay as still as the dead, immobilised by fear, until the truck rolled out of the carpark and headed up the road. Both she and Grace poked their heads above the thistles. The truck pulled into some trees further up the road and the engine was cut. Two doors slammed, one after the other.

'They're hiding the brumby while they go back to the pub,' whispered Grace.

'We have to warn your mum!' Jess looked to the tree above. 'Give me a boost. I'll see if I can get phone coverage higher up!'

Grace cupped her hands for Jess to step into. Jess hoisted herself up into the tree and climbed as high as she could. Grace followed. From the top, they could see the two runners heading for the pub.

'Can you get a signal?' whispered Grace.

Jess opened her phone. 'Yep.' She immediately began thumbing a message to Mrs Arnold.

Brumby runners about to walk into pub!

Within seconds the phone buzzed in Jess's hand.

Where are you?
Outside window. Up tree.

Someone lifted the sash window.

'Hoo-hooo!' Grace did her best owl impersonation.

Mrs Arnold waved briefly, slammed the window shut and vanished. At virtually the same moment, the runners disappeared into the building.

Near the road, the foal cried again, and some other horses from surrounding farms whinnied back. Jess slipped down the main trunk of the tree.

'Where are you going?' hissed Grace.

'To help that brumby,' answered Jess. 'Coming?'

'What about Mum?'

'She can look after herself,' said Jess, taking off along the road.

15

'WHAT ABOUT THE DOGS?' said Grace, panting as she tried to keep up with Jess's strides.

'They'll be chained up,' said Jess. 'Come on!'

'Are you nuts? Those dogs will eat us.'

'They're only pups.'

'Only pups?' Grace squeaked. 'Big pups!'

Jess found a good, thick branch, then kept walking towards the truck. As they got closer the dogs started to bark. Jess had never heard a noise so loud or ferocious. She silently thanked God the two dogs weren't fully grown, and mimicked their owner's voice as best she could. *'Max! Brutus! Siddown and shuddup!'*

The dogs backed off and, to Jess's immense relief, lay down, snarling quietly. *'Siddownnnn,'* Jess growled again. She raised the thick branch at them. Both dogs cowered.

She wrenched open the driver's side door. 'The key is still in the ignition!' She looked back at Grace, who was hanging back nervously. 'You drive better than I do.'

'Jess! I'm only fifteen. I can't drive on a road.'

'So we'll go through the paddocks.'

'Where to?'

'Back to the mountains,' said Jess, sliding into the front of the truck. 'Come on, quick!' She groped around with her feet, trying to find the pedals. 'Which one makes it go?'

'You have to turn it on first, derrr.' Grace appeared by the door. 'Move over!'

Jess slid over and let Grace slip in behind the wheel. Her friend sat on the edge of the seat and groped for the keys.

'Can you reach the pedals?'

'Nup.' Grace slid half off the seat and kicked around with her feet.

The keys jangled and the engine suddenly roared as Grace hit the accelerator too hard. Jess fumbled around on the bench seat, finding crushed empty beer cans and other unidentifiable things. She ran her hand over a hard cylindrical object – a torch. She flicked it on.

'No wonder it stinks in here,' she said. At her feet, bathed in torchlight, was something that looked like a dead rabbit. She pulled the front of her jumper up over her mouth and nose.

'Throw it to the dogs. It might shut them up,' said Grace.

Jess found an old shirt and wrapped it around her hand, then picked the animal up by two stiff back legs. She tossed it to Max and Brutus. 'There you go, boys,' she said in her runner's voice. *'Don't say I never give yez nuffin.'*

The sounds of growling and crunching of bones gave Jess the shivers and she wound the window up to shut out the noise as the two dogs fought over the putrid carcass.

'Go to Matty's Creek,' she said. 'We'll try to get back to the mountains from there.'

'Can't you go any faster?' asked Jess.

'I can't reach the clutch to change gears,' said Grace, gripping the steering wheel with both hands. 'We're stuck in first gear. Besides, we can't put the headlights on or someone will see us.'

'This is so illegal,' said Jess, suddenly having an attack of conscience.

The truck suddenly lurched. 'No, it's not, because I'm not actually driving on the road. I'm on private property . . . sort of.'

'We stole a truck!'

'We're just borrowing it. I don't think it's even registered; there's no sticker.' Grace peered into the rear-view mirror. 'Besides, this was *your* idea, remember? How's the brumby going?'

Jess wasn't sure how the lack of rego made things any more or less legal. She peered back through the cabin window. The small horse stood in the crate with its legs wide and head high. 'It seems okay. Wonder what happened to its mum.'

'Let's hope she's back in the mountains,' said Grace, continuing into the darkness. Before long, the truck lurched towards the river crossing.

'This is where Luke's mum died,' said Jess quietly as the truck rumbled onto the timber bridge. As the words left her mouth, the sound of screaming rushed down the channel of the river bed, carried by a low, moaning wind. The brumby foal answered with a piercing cry that caught Jess by the lungs and stopped her breathing. The torch went out. The truck jerked to a stop.

'Damn, stalled it,' said Grace, reaching for the keys. 'Turn that torch back on.'

'I'm trying,' said Jess.

Everything went silent for a few moments. Then a tiny breeze wafted in through the cabin and ran over Jess's cheek, gently lifting the hair from around her ear and dropping it back down again. She gave the torch a shake and got a weak beam. She shivered.

'How weird was that?' she whispered.

'Too weird,' answered Grace in a nervous voice as she kicked the truck back into life.

The sky had thickened with cloud, obscuring the moon. The night was dark and drizzly. 'Where are the windscreen wipers?' said Grace. She fiddled with a few levers. 'Must be broken.'

Grace continued driving slowly along the side of the road, her elbow and head hanging out the window, one hand on the wheel, until eventually they reached Matty's Creek.

'Now what are we going to do with this horse?' asked Jess, as Grace stopped the truck at the forty-four-gallon drum by the front gate. All she could see of the kangaroos was their red eyes, gleaming in the darkness.

'Put it in with Dodger and Legsy?' suggested Grace.

'It's a brumby. It'll just injure itself trying to get past the fences. We've got to get it back to the mountains.' Jess sighed. 'How will it find its mother? We haven't even checked to see if it's injured.' She put her hand to her forehead and groaned. 'Oh God, this was such a dumb idea.' She got out and slammed the car door.

The dogs snarled, low and menacing, and Jess growled back. *'Siddown, bunny-breath!'*

She ran her torch over the brumby and it jumped and shied at the beams of light. 'Easy now,' she said, switching to a soft tone while running the torch up and down its trembling legs. It was a filly. Jess was relieved to find it had no injuries. It called loudly and desperately into the darkness. As Jess shone the torch over its face she saw Sapphire's wild blue eyes staring back at her, icy-blue and hauntingly human. 'We can't just let her go. Dingos will get her.'

Grace got out and unlatched the gate. 'Let's try driving the same way we went today. We can follow Mum's tyre marks.'

She turned on the headlights and the house lit up before them. The kangaroos fell away from the light in panic, bounding over the fence and into the hills in one big hopping mob. In the sheep yard, Dodger and Legsy nickered.

Grace drove the truck towards the creek crossing and stopped. 'Reckon we can get through?' she asked, with her head out the window. 'I reckon it's risen since this arvo.'

'It was up to the horses' elbows today,' answered Jess. 'I don't think this old beast is gonna get through it.'

'Maybe we should just take her home,' said Grace.

'To Coachwood? Harry's?'

'Yeah, why not? Sapphire's mares are there. They might adopt her.'

Jess's mind filled with the image of the big creamy stallion, so traumatised by the brumby-runners, pacing frantically about the yards at Harry's. And his dead body being dragged down the laneway behind a tractor, never to return to his mountains again. 'It would be better to leave her here,' she said. 'Anyway, there's no room on the float. We have to get Dodger and Legsy home.'

The brumby on the back cried out. A deep old nicker from somewhere up on the hillside answered.

'*Rambo!*' the girls chorused.

Jess stuck her head out the window and called to him. 'Hey, old man!' She couled hear the old horse ambling slowly towards them, his legs brushing the long grass.

Jess unclipped the dogs and dragged them, growling and snapping, to the horse float and locked them in the back, tipping half a bag of Filth and Fang's dog biscuits in after them. Then she ran back to the truck and shone the torch over the stock crate, looking for the handles. She swung the doors open, then joined Grace in the front of the truck.

Rambo waded through the shoulder-deep river and emerged at the same steady pace, the river dripping from his feathered legs, droplets of light rain rolling through his shaggy forelock and shimmering as it caught the lights of the truck.

He whickered gently to the terrified filly and it bleated back in pathetically grateful whinnies.

Rambo lifted his nose to the back of the truck, exchanged sniffs with the small horse, then turned and walked away. The brumby stood trembling at the mouth of the cage, ears pressed back against her skull. In a sudden burst of bravery, she leapt after the old black horse, landed on awkward legs and toppled over. She recovered quickly and gambolled to Rambo as though she knew him, leaping and rearing and paddling her legs at the old horse's shoulders.

Jess watched the pale shape of the filly dancing around Rambo's larger black outline in the shafts of light. 'Let's call her Min Min,' she said. 'After the min min lights.'

'Beautiful,' smiled Grace.

The two horses disappeared into the shadows. Jess heard their hooves knocking the rocks against each other, stone clacking against stone as they dislodged them. There was a splash, silence for a moment, then pebbles knocking on the other side of the river. Overhead, the trees murmured and swayed in the wind and the sound swallowed the two horses as they climbed up the mountain and into the night.

'I think she'll be okay now,' said Grace.

But Jess was already thinking of the next hurdle. 'We'd better get this truck back.'

'Can't we just roll it into the river?'

'It's not deep enough,' grinned Jess, although she quite liked the idea. 'And we have to get back to the pub with those dumb dogs.'

The carpark was full when they got back to the pub; a mix of utes, four-wheel drives and stock trucks.

Grace and Jess returned the runners' truck with Max and Brutus locked inside the stock crate. They clambered back up the flooded gum and sat side-by-side on a thick branch, like a pair of tawny owls, overlooking the pub.

Jess huddled into her jacket and braced her shoulders against the wind. Her jeans were wet, and her knees knocked together with cold. As her phone picked up a signal again, it buzzed with about twenty frantic messages from Mrs Arnold, demanding to know where they had got to. Jess balanced precariously on the tree branch, one eye on the pub, the other on her phone.

The doors opened and the voices coming from inside sounded dispirited. People began filing out, speaking in low grumbles. Mrs Arnold's voice still rang loud and obnoxious from inside.

'I reckon Queensland must be winning,' said Grace.

'Yep, all over for New South Wales, by the looks of it,' said Jess. 'Can you see the runners?'

'Yeah,' said Grace, suddenly surprised. 'They're drinking with Mum. Look!'

They could see Mrs Arnold standing by a tall bar

table, raising a schooner of port to the two men they had met on the mountain. They looked like old friends. Mrs Arnold had a maroon beanie on her head and seemed to be singing.

'Oh no,' groaned Grace. 'Mum's on the turps with them.'

Jess didn't answer. 'Hey, isn't that Barker's wagon?'

The white police wagon was parked sneakily behind a bend in the road, just shy of the pub.

'Luke must be back.' Jess kept scrolling through her messages and found several from Luke.

Filth okay, just bruising.
Back at pub. Where are you?
Jess, you OK?

She messaged him back.

Look in the tree out the window. What is Mrs A doing???

Within moments, Luke's lanky figure appeared on the balcony of the pub and he peered out into the darkness.

'*Hooo-hooo!*' called Jess, doing another bad owl impression.

Grace started the *Koo-koo-kaaa* of a kookaburra and abruptly choked on it as Jess elbowed her in the ribs. 'That's a *morning* bird, Gracie!'

Luke slipped through the beer garden and out into the dripping wet paddock. Jess noticed his sling was gone. 'How's your arm?' she asked when he reached the foot of the tree.

'No fracture,' he said, breathless and smiling. 'It's just the old injury giving me grief. The vet wrapped it for me.' He held up his arm. Below the cuff of his jacket his hand was wrapped in a thick blue bandage. Using his good hand, he grabbed hold of a lower limb and climbed up beside Jess. 'Those runners are plastered. Mrs A's got them totally hammered.'

He unravelled a footy scarf from around his neck and wrapped it around Jess's, then sat with his legs either side of the limb and put both arms around her shoulders. As he spoke, his warm breath brushed over her ears. 'Barker's just waiting for them. He's gonna nab them as soon as they get in their truck.'

'Lucky we brought it back, then,' said Grace.

'Huh?'

Jess and Grace filled him in on their journey with Min Min. The runners finally emerged, staggering through the doors of the pub. Mrs Arnold was visible through the window, slumped over the bar table.

They sat, grinning, as they watched the runners stagger to their truck and look, puzzled, into the back of the crate as they registered that the horse was gone.

The runners scratched their heads at the dogs locked in the back, then finally got into the truck. They pulled out onto the road without switching their headlights on. Within seconds, Barker's police car lit up in a pretty show of blue and red flashing lights as he pulled them over. Jess, Grace and Luke watched gleefully as the men were put in the back of the wagon with their dogs and driven away.

'This is better than watching the footy,' laughed Grace. She jumped down out of the tree.

Luke slipped down after her and held his arms up for Jess. She fell into them and couldn't help stealing a kiss on the way down.

'Brumbies one, runners nil!' said Grace, skipping happily back towards the pub.

16

JESS WOKE the next morning to the sound of Mrs Arnold snoring. Sunlight bled through the tiny slit in the curtains, and she could hear staff bustling around the kitchen as they prepared pub lunches.

'What time is it?' Jess rolled over and looked at her watch. *'Eleven o'clock!'* She sat up and the bed swung beneath her like a hammock. 'We'll have to leave soon. Mum and Dad are expecting me home tonight!'

Luke was back at his property, and Mrs Arnold . . . Jess immediately began doing sums in her head. If she could get Mrs Arnold conscious within an hour, the seven-hour drive might get her home before dark . . . if she really pushed it. 'Hell!'

Jess glanced across the room at a lump of purple chenille with a maroon beanie and messy black curls at one end, steel-capped boots hanging out the other. The bedspread rose and fell with each snore.

'I've got no hope,' said Jess.

She caught her image in the mirror over the small dresser. Her chin was red with stubble rash. She felt Luke's lips over hers again, closed her eyes and melted into the memory of her back pressing against the flooded gum, his breath on her skin. She couldn't remember ever finding it so hard to tear herself away from a cold, wet paddock in the middle of the night. But the rain had come down more heavily and soon they had been forced inside.

Luke had laughed at her chattering teeth and led her to the warmth of the pub fire. Kitty had locked up the bar and left them there, declaring them family and telling them to leave via the kitchen door when they felt like it.

'Family,' Kitty had called Luke. 'A local.' And although her heart warmed to see him so embraced by a community of people, Jess also felt a nagging fear, which she tried to ignore. Coachwood Crossing had been his home, but now he had an entire community in another state, hours away.

From the purple chenille came a low moan. *'Carrrnnn the mighty maroons . . .'*

'Oh God, you're still drunk,' said Grace, appearing in the doorway.

'Wasn't my fault,' murmured Mrs Arnold. 'It was for a noble cause. Oh Lordy, my head.' An arm flopped down the side of the saggy bed, then there was no further movement. She began snoring again.

'Very noble,' said Grace, looking down her nose at her mother.

'I told my parents I'd be back for dinner,' said Jess, hurriedly stuffing her things into her bag. She had to get home. Any more misadventures would jeopardise the entire brumby arrangement with her parents.

As she spoke, Luke appeared in the doorway, breathless. 'There are more brumby-runners up in the hills, heaps of them. I just overheard in the dunnies. There's a big run on today.'

Jess's heart missed a beat. 'What?'

'We've got to stop them,' Luke panted.

'How?' said Jess, reaching for her jeans and pulling them on over her boxers. 'I have to be back in Coachwood Crossing by the end of the day.'

Luke glanced around the room. His gaze settled on Mrs Arnold. 'Ask Mrs Arnold. Wake her up.'

'*You* wake her up,' said Grace.

Luke went momentarily silent. 'She wouldn't be able to drive you home anyway, the state she's in.'

'I thought *you* were going to drive me home,' said Jess.

He groaned. 'Won't your parents give you one more day?'

'No way, school tomorrow. Luke, I promised them. *You* promised them.'

'There are people running brumbies up on the mountain right now. What do you want to do? It's your call.' He looked anxious, one foot out the door. She could see him silently praying for the answer he wanted.

Jess grabbed her jacket. 'Okay. Let's go. We'll sort the rest out later.'

Luke instantly vanished from the doorway. Grace scrawled a note for her comatose mother as Jess ran after him.

Jess dived into the back of the ute, grabbed the roll bar and felt the car lurch into gear. Grace tumbled in beside her. Luke sent the car fishtailing over the gravelly road and they hurtled towards Matty's Creek.

17

GRACE AND JESS leapt from the back of the ute, bridles in hand, before it even came to a stop. They had the horses' rugs unbuckled in seconds. Luke jumped the fence, carrying the saddles.

'Double with me,' Jess said to Grace, pulling Dodger's girth tight and slapping the fender down. She hoisted herself into the saddle and Grace vaulted on behind. Jess kicked Dodger through the opened gate and Luke cantered on Legsy behind them.

They splashed through the river and opened the horses into a full gallop across the hillside, wads of mud flying up from the thundering hooves.

'Which way do we go?' yelled Grace as they neared the top of the hill.

'I don't know,' called Luke. 'Let's start at the same spot as yesterday, go from there.'

Jess guided Dodger up the steep, narrow trail and he

bounded over the ruts and rocks, puffing heavily. 'Good boy, Dodge,' she encouraged, clicking him up.

At the top of the hill, she let him walk.

'I can hear them,' said Luke, pulling a jig-jogging Legsy up beside her. 'Listen, the brumbies are going nuts.'

Dodger pranced nervously and flicked his ears. Jess picked up the faint drumming sound too. She ran a soothing hand over her horse's neck. 'How can we stop them?'

There was a sudden ear-piercing scream and a pounding of hooves.

'A stallion!' yelled Grace. 'Really close!' She twisted to look behind her. 'It's Rambo!' she said joyously.

The big black horse came charging through a wall of bushes, whinnying and tossing his head. He pranced on the spot and for a moment Jess could see wildness raging inside him. She saw a glimpse of what he had been in his youth, an animal with a proud crest and high-stepping knees. His tail swished angrily back and forth, and with a shake of his mane he was off, cantering in another direction, disappearing into a field of granite boulders.

They guided the horses carefully down into a gully littered with rotting logs, travelling as quickly as safety would allow. Dodger pulled at the reins and Jess had trouble holding him steady.

Rambo's shape flickered through the bush, disappearing behind massive granite boulders and then reappearing across the gully. He backtracked every now and then, sighted them, and then charged off again.

'We can't lose him,' said Luke, overtaking Jess and pushing Legsy into a canter. But Jess held Dodger at a jog.

Around them, the sound of drumming hooves grew louder and echoed off the rocks and through the canyons and valleys, shaking the branches of the beech trees and sending their leaves spiralling to the trails below. Jess heard a whip crack.

'We should stop,' said Grace in a frightened voice. 'He's leading us into the chase. It's too dangerous.'

Jess was about to agree when she heard a heartbreaking sound. A foal screaming.

Ahead, Luke yelled '*Jessy!*' The anguish in his tone made her push on even faster. Dodger scrambled to a ridge-top and the sight before Jess nearly tore her to pieces. 'Min Min!'

Slung between two trees, like a huge spider web, was a net. Snared in that net, like helpless prey, was a distraught creamy foal. Beside it, Rambo pawed at the ground and shook his head. 'Min Min!' Jess yelled.

'There are more,' said Luke, pointing to two other nets strung nearby. 'They're gonna run the whole mob through here!'

'What can we do?' she said desperately.

Luke threw her a pocket knife. 'You cut her out. I'll head off the chase.'

Jess slipped off Dodger. 'You go too,' she said breathlessly to Grace. 'We can't let them through here.' But she paused before letting go of the reins. 'Take care of my boy.'

Grace nodded solemnly before leapfrogging into the saddle and reining Dodger away at a steady lope.

Jess set to work on the net, the sound of the chase all around her. Rambo ran his soft muzzle over the neck of the distressed foal, nickering gently. Min Min lay motionless, but her eyes rolled and her cries still came, each one tearing at Jess's heart and filling her with urgency. She worked quietly and quickly, sawing at the nylon strings tangled around the foal's entire body. Her struggling had only entangled her further. Jess hacked and sawed, pulled and stretched, until finally she tugged the last shred of net away from the filly's back legs.

For a split second, Jess, Min Min and Rambo were collectively motionless. Then Rambo turned and trotted away. The filly leapt to her feet and scooted after him with her tail jammed hard between her legs.

Another whip crack spurred Jess to the next net, tied high between the trunks of two trees. She could cut just one side, she thought quickly, cut it from the top and peel it back, clear the way for the brumbies. With the knife in her teeth, she took hold of the net and pushed her boots into the lower holes, pulling herself up.

From the top, as she cut through the holding rope, she spied the runners, their fleeting shapes moving through the bush. Horses flashed in and out of sight. Then they disappeared into the forest, calling to each other with the excitement and adrenaline of the chase.

The galloping brumbies sent a current of terror ringing through the mountain. They pounded through the grey gums and stringybarks, getting closer. The hooves of the chasing horses clattered over rocks.

Jess sawed desperately at the ropes. She had to hurry. She heard Luke's voice, yelling. As she looked up, she felt the last shred of rope give. Then everything went blurry around her, her vision replaced by shock and disorientation, a falling sensation. A fraction of a second later she felt the impact of her shoulder crashing against stone, and her head thudding onto the ground.

Around her the forest floor still rumbled with the rolling hoofbeats of the brumbies. They faded as she drifted away, into unconsciousness.

18

JESS WOKE to a broad, cushiony muzzle pushing into the small of her back. There was a quiet rumble, and then she felt the hard bone of horse's nose nudging her.

She opened her eyes and groaned at the nauseating dullness that filled her head. As her vision sharpened she saw a heavily feathered hoof scraping at the ground in front of her. Above her, Rambo looked impatient.

She closed her eyes again and winced as she tried to move her arm. It worked, she realised with relief, but it hurt.

Rambo turned and walked away.

'Wait,' she croaked, trying to pull herself up.

The big horse clomped away, his rump swinging from side to side.

Jess stood, nursing her arm. All around, the forest looked the same. She was in some kind of deep gully, with shrubs so thick she couldn't see beyond a couple of metres.

The sky was overcast and she couldn't tell east from west, north from south.

'Don't leave me,' she called to Rambo, but his pace only quickened.

'Rambo, wait!'

When she caught up with him he stopped and bent his neck around in an arc, placing his head low. She stood to the side of him, put both arms over his neck and let him toss her up. His round back was as broad as a couch under her aching legs. Relieved, she curled her fingers around his mane. Rambo wheeled away at a trot. She didn't know where he was taking her, but he seemed to be in a hurry.

Rambo's shoulders dropped suddenly and Jess grabbed at his mane as he plunged into a steeply carved creek bed. Rocks clacked against each other as the big horse found his footing. Jess pushed away the spiky wattle leaves and leaned along his neck, pressing her face into his mane and moving her arms forward to feel the steady thrust of his shoulders.

Beyond the creek, there was movement in the bush. Rambo's chest rumbled quietly. Soon they were joined by a small brown mare and a matching foal. Other mares, some pregnant, some with young ones, dropped down into the creek bed, pushing a break along the hidden route. No foal cried and no mare whinnied. Barely a branch or twig snapped or a stone turned beneath their hooves. There was just a soft swishing of moving branches, and the steady billowing of the brumbies breathing.

The brumbies travelled like this for nearly an hour until they reached a tiny beach of gravel on the edge of a small pool. Massive, angular columns of rock rose above them. Jess gazed up in awe.

And there the brumbies stopped. They rested as a tight herd, seven mares plus assorted foals, against the tall cliff of jagged granite that rose, perfectly vertical, for hundreds of metres. They were barricaded in by a wall of undergrowth, ti-tree and wattle so dense that Jess wondered how she would ever get out of there. The words of Matilda's stories floated through her mind.

In a landlocked valley, deeply secret, wild and unclaimed . . .

Jess could hear nothing but the soft breathing of the horses, the wall of stone before them blocking out all other sound. Still, not one of the horses nickered or moved. They stood evenly on four feet, breathing quietly, ears flickering back and forth . . . waiting . . . listening.

When Jess slipped quietly from Rambo's back they startled, and looked ready to run again. She crouched low, so as not to frighten them. There were palominos and buckskins, creamies and chestnuts, all mares and foals, all staring at her with either one or two blue eyes. Jess felt the skin prickle on the back of her neck.

Saladin's spirit is born to the blue-eyed brumbies . . .
It was a peculiar feeling, having all those eyes staring at her. And she sensed that there were more, hiding, silent, in other small pockets nearby. Jess crept on her hands and knees under the dense scrub and found a small, grassy clearing. Three small brown foals lay curled together with a mare standing over them. Babies. This place was a nursery. She sighed at the wondrousness of it.

The place, so exquisitely special, must be kept secret.
But where was their stallion, she wondered? Were they Sapphire's mares? Or had they belonged to the big golden stallion at the saleyards?

The mare turned an ear towards Jess and lifted her nose. Jess backed away and let the branches fold back, hiding her from the foals again.

As she looked at the brumbies, huddled closely to-gether, she thought of her own horses. They had nowhere near the craftiness of the brumbies, their ability to slither through the bush as though they were a part of it. In a campdraft arena, Dodger was as sure-footed as they came, but through bush like this, he didn't come close to the brumbies for stealth.

She thought of Grace riding him and suddenly had an uneasy feeling in her gut. What if Dodger went down a wombat hole, what if he stumbled onto rocks, or galloped off a cliff? He didn't know this country. She silently prayed that he was okay.

Jess looked up at the purple, swirling clouds above and hoped it wouldn't snow again. How long should she stay down here, in this secret place? She saw there were cracks in the stone above her and it looked as though the cliff might be fairly easy to climb. She took a deep breath and grabbed at a handhold.

The rock was hard and cold, it had no softness to it at all, and she realised it was going to hurt if she fell. A lot. But what choice did she have? No one would find her here; she had to find a way out for herself.

She squeezed inside the narrow gap in front of her and winced when she bumped her hip against a jagged piece of rock. Yep. This was gonna hurt. She kept going, finding a hold, pulling and reaching up with the opposite foot at the same time, ignoring the pain in her arm and keeping the momentum going as much as she could. She knew that once she stopped and had to haul her weight with her arms it would sap her strength, so she kept reaching out, looking for holds, pushing up with her legs and not looking down.

Jess kept climbing until she could barely breathe and

a stitch threatened to split her ribs apart. The muscles in her arms and legs burned, but she forced them to keep going until the light lifted and she realised that she was rising above the trees and out of their shadow.

Still she did not look down. Up, up, she went, until she could see the tussocky grasses at the top coming closer. Her legs trembled with fatigue. She was scared they might seize up totally. Small plants grew from the rock, so much softer on her hands and so easy to hold, but she resisted the temptation. If they uprooted she would surely plummet to her death.

Finally, Jess dragged herself onto the top of the cliff and rolled onto her side, chest heaving, heart slamming so hard that she couldn't move.

She closed her eyes and sucked in the biggest gulps of air she could, to soothe her body, feed it with oxygen, calm it and steady her pulse. For a good ten minutes she lay there, eyes closed, with barely the strength to roll over.

It was her mobile phone that finally roused her. A buzz and rumble. A text message. Without getting up, she shifted and pulled it from her pocket. It was from her mum.

Can you stop and get some milk on the way home?

Jess crawled to the edge and looked down. Not far below, the horses were gone. The secret place, it seemed, had closed its leafy doors behind her and it was as though it had never existed. She sat, feeling slightly dazed, and thumbed a reply:

I might be a bit late.

Jess walked away from the cliff face, past stringybarks and grey gums and through broken and parted under-growth. She found hoof prints stamped on the churned-up forest floor. She followed them, down through a gully and onto a ridge. From there, she looked out over a wide, grassy hollow, dotted with twisting white eucalypts.

There was an explosive crack, and the surrounding hillside suddenly came alive with movement, flashes of white and the steady beat of hooves.

A coloured mare cantered across the open country. She was old and scarred, thin, with a greying brown face. Her brown-and-white sides were wet with sweat and she carried her head low. Beside her ran a knobbly-legged foal, and two blue dogs growled and snapped at her heels. Three horsemen followed, in mustering hats and oilskin jackets, whips cracking alongside their mounts. Their horses were tall and fit and eager, driving the exhausted mare until she could no longer continue.

She came to a stop and stood there heaving, eyes closed, head drooping, while her foal cried and butted and circled her.

The riders tossed ropes around her head and neck and pulled them tight. She was the weakest of the mob, the easiest to catch, but the runners were taking her anyway.

The men and their dogs kept pushing the wretched horse along the flat, in and out of the strappy-leaved lomandra grasses and granite boulders that littered the misty hollow.

Jess followed silently along the ridge-top, watching. What she witnessed next made her boil with anger.

19

A SMALL TRUCK, patched with rust and carrying a stock crate, rolled over the open grassland towards the three riders. A man got out and sprang onto the back of the truck. As it drove alongside the mare, he reached over and slung another heavy coiled rope around her neck, pulling it tight until her face was pressed against the side of the tray.

The truck stopped while he reached for her tail. He grabbed it and pulled it in, so hard that the mare was nearly torn from her feet. She struggled and kicked, but the half-hitched knots around her throat and tail only tightened, bending her body into an arc.

Jess watched in horror as the foal was roped with a slipknot around its neck and then hooked to a small motorised device at the back of the crate. There was a grating noise as the winch slowly dragged the struggling foal to the opening of the crate.

There was no ramp or step. The foal was dragged by the throat off the ground, its stalky legs paddling wildly, knocking against the metal corners of the crate and banging against the doorway. Its body was dragged across the tray. A man jumped in after it and knelt on its neck while he loosened the rope. Jess could see its body heaving to get air back into its lungs.

The man lashed the rope around the side of the cage before allowing the foal to struggle to its feet. Then he pulled it to the side of the cage and tied it there. The man hopped out, slammed the cage doors and sat on the back of the truck with his feet dangling. The vehicle rolled slowly across the grassy hollow with the mare scrambling awkwardly alongside, the riders trotting their horses along behind it.

Jess sank to the ground, too dispirited to see another vehicle rumble out of the forest, flanked by several more riders and a huge black wolf dog.

The frenzied barking and yelling that ensued snapped her out of her hopelessness.

'Mrs Arnold!' Jess watched her step out of the fourbie. Another, newer four-wheel drive appeared from the forest behind it. Two men stepped out in full police uniform. 'Barker!' Jess ran to them. Among the riders she could see Kitty and Steve, and some other locals from the pub.

Luke was off his horse, struggling to hold onto Fang.

The big dog's hackles stood on end and he fought so hard to get free, Jess was sure that he'd kill someone if Luke let go. The runners' dogs, propped on all fours, howled back.

'Hey!' Jess broke into a run. 'Guys!'

There was a sharp whistle and the blue dogs suddenly sprinted away. The runners wheeled their horses around and spurred them on, fleeing to the cover of the forest. The runners' truck lurched suddenly to one side, taking the mare's feet out from under her as it revved loudly into a U-turn. The mare scrambled desperately to regain a foothold.

'Cut her loose!' Jess heard the driver yell. The man on the back crawled across the tray and began furiously sawing at her ropes. He freed her tail first, then cut the neck rope. The truck bumped over the ground faster and faster. The mare toppled over, landing heavily on her side, her legs flailing.

On the truck the foal screamed for its mother. The cage doors were flung open and it tumbled to the ground, flipping end over end in a tangle of limbs.

'You low-life *pigs*,' Jess yelled as she ran.

With a flying leap, Luke sprang into the saddle. He kicked Legsy into a gallop, not stopping for stirrups. Fang raced alongside him. Kitty and Steve followed and they disappeared into the forest amid a drumming of hoofbeats and echoing yells. Barker's car bumped wildly over the grassy flat, going after the runners' truck.

Mrs Arnold beat Jess to the mare and held a hand up, telling Jess to stop. She crouched down beside the mare's body. It didn't move. Not an ear twitched. The rise and fall of the horse's sides was the only clue that there was still life inside her. Mrs Arnold waved Jess over.

'Look through my car and see if you can find any sort of wound spray,' she said. 'And get that purple bedspread too.'

'Did you steal the bedspread *again*?'

'They're handy things, haven't you worked that out yet?' Mrs Arnold hissed back. 'Go. Go. Before she tries to get up!'

Jess raced to the car, where Grace held Dodger.

'Is she going to die?' asked Grace.

'I don't know. She's completely shut down. Your mum asked for wound spray.' Jess paused to run her eyes over Dodger, leg by leg, shoulder, hips, neck, face . . .

'He pulled a shoe,' said Grace quickly. 'But otherwise he's fine. Try in the glovebox.'

Jess flung open the glovebox and began unceremoniously tossing out papers and plastic crap. 'Antiseptic cream! Perfect!'

'The foal is over there, behind the trees,' said Grace. 'It was limping.'

'Okay, good. Don't lose sight of it.'

Mrs Arnold had two hands on the mare's neck. 'You hold her neck firmly down, you hear me? Do not let her lift her head or she'll kick mine off my shoulders.' She eyeballed Jess. 'Got it?'

Jess placed her hands on the mare's neck and lightly rested one knee on her as well, just in case. Mrs Arnold took the cream and began smearing it all over the cuts on the mare's tail and over the wounds on her neck. When she had finished, she took the purple chenille and began rolling it up into a long floppy sausage. She slid it under the mare's neck.

'Help me pull her up,' said Mrs Arnold, handing Jess one end.

Together they pulled and pulled until the mare lifted her head.

'Come on, old girl. Get up or the dingos will get you.' Mrs Arnold heaved again. 'Come on, darlin'.'

The mare put one leg out in front of her.

'Good girl. Let her rest a minute.'

Jess stood quietly next to Mrs Arnold, waiting.

The mare rolled back onto the ground and groaned.

'No, no you don't!' Mrs Arnold began pulling again, harder this time. 'You have to get up,' she said angrily. She kicked at the mare with her boot and yelled at her. *'Gwan, get up!'* She yanked mercilessly at the bedspread.

From the trees the foal gave a frightened whinny. With

a final surge of effort, the mare struggled to her feet and Jess and Mrs Arnold jumped back. She stood on shaky legs, looking dazed. She had skin off all over.

Mrs Arnold cursed under her breath. 'Sweet Jesus, what have they done to you?'

'We need Rambo,' said Jess. 'He'll take care of her.' She took off for the rock platform, bounding through the swampy grasses, her boots squelching and sucking at the mud.

At the platform she leaned over into the gully below and called as loud as she could.

'Rambo!'

'Rambo!'

'RAMBO!'

She didn't know how many times she screamed his name.

While they waited, they ushered the mare to the shelter of some trees and let her be. They shut themselves in the car and watched for the foal to come to her. She gave one small nicker and her baby emerged and began suckling from her, butting and nuzzling anxiously.

'There you go, you little squirt,' said Grace, watching through the back window of the car.

It seemed hours before the big old horse came clumping out of the grey gums. He did little, but stood close by, keeping an ear turned towards the mare and her foal.

'She's just so exhausted,' said Mrs Arnold. 'Rambo will take care of her until she's rested up.'

'Wish I could give her a bucket of water,' said Jess.

'She wouldn't take it.'

'Yeah, I know.'

Rambo lifted his head and the foal started anxiously rubbing up against his mother again.

Luke rode out of the trees with Kitty and Steve alongside. Something about the way they sat in their saddles told Jess they'd been triumphant.

'Barker's got the truck driver and his sidekick in handcuffs,' Luke said as he pulled Legsy to a stop. 'The riders got away, though. They rode like maniacs.'

'You did the right thing pulling up. Not worth wrecking your good horse,' said Mrs Arnold. 'They'll keep.'

They gathered by Mrs Arnold's car as Barker's white fourbie rolled up the hillside and onto the grassy flat. As it went past, Jess could see the two men in the back, with their hands cuffed. They weren't the runners they had met the day before.

'What, is there some sort of national brumby-running convention on up here or something?' Mrs Arnold stared in through the car window. 'How many of you grubs are there?'

The men snarled and said nothing.

Barker winked and kept driving. Mrs Arnold began

slowly clapping as they drove off. Grace joined her and together they cheered and waved to the brumby-runners as they were escorted off the mountain.

'I hope that's the last we see of them,' said Luke.

'Scum,' muttered Jess, as they disappeared from sight.

20

LUKE RODE OVER TO Jess and leaned down. 'Ride home with me?'

'Sure,' said Jess, picking up Dodger's reins. She grinned. This was an exceptionally beautiful place for a ride.

'I want to come too,' said Grace. 'Give us a leg up, will you?'

'Dodger might be a bit tired,' said Jess, giving her a meaningful look.

'Oh.' Grace rolled her eyes and reached for the car door. 'See you back at the pub then, I s'pose.'

'We'll come down through Matty's Creek,' said Luke. 'Be back before dark.'

'Be careful,' said Mrs Arnold. 'Those other riders are still out here somewhere.'

'They'll be long gone,' said Luke. 'They headed in the other direction, back through the state forest.'

Mrs Arnold pulled a rolled-up oilskin from the car.

'Take my Driza-Bone. You might need it.'

Jess followed Luke back over the crest of the mountain, where the wind howled remorselessly. She pressed the studs of the Driza-Bone together, fastening it around her, and enjoyed the way the wind made the skin on her face burn. She looked out over the endless waves of gorges and ridge-tops, and felt her chest fill with something wonderful.

Dark clouds rolled over the mountains and the cold began to seep through the oilskin. 'It's going to snow again,' she said, excitedly.

'Or bucket with rain,' said Luke. He pushed Legsy into a trot.

As they rode into the open woodlands, the wind shook the raindrops from the leathery leaves and ribbon bark flapped around enormous white tree trunks. Branches creaked and splintered above them. Moss hung from the trees like old grey beards.

They went deeper into gorges where creeks cut invisible channels beneath carpets of ferns and tangled sticks. It was slow going, and all the while the wind followed them, like whispering voices carrying ancient secrets.

In front of them a wombat trundled along a narrow trail, then disappeared into its burrow. Further ahead, kangaroos grazed in pockets of wetlands and bush birds twittered in the flowering heath.

They pushed through tangled vine thickets and made

their way deeper into the gully. She-oaks swished above the beaches of gravel beside the creek bed and Jess heard the soft *clik-clik* of cockatoos breaking the cones, husking the seeds and letting the caffs fall to the ground beneath them.

'Look, there's an old track,' said Luke. There was a narrow parting in the trees, and grass grew knee-high between them.

'It goes the wrong way,' said Jess.

'Let's follow it anyway.'

Fat drops of rain splatted onto Jess's oilskin. 'I think we should just get to Matty's Creek.'

'Come on, let's just have a quick look.' Luke pushed Legsy into a slow canter and Jess reluctantly let Dodger follow.

The track became wider but the grass was still thick as they cantered along it. A little further on, the track stopped at a wide, grassy flat. At the edge of the flat was a small hut. It was made from stone and slabs of wood and old scraps of corrugated iron. It was little more than a box with a chimney.

'Oh, wow!' said Luke, dismounting and tying Legsy to a tree. Jess tethered Dodger and followed Luke into the hut.

It was tiny inside, barely big enough for a rolled-out swag, and there wasn't even a window, but it was dry, and the rain was starting to pelt down. Jess pulled off the Driza-Bone and tossed it in a wet pile on the floor. The stone fireplace had a steel rod through it and an old pot hung in the hearth. Next to it was a bundle of dry wood.

'Let's make billy tea!' said Luke, like an excited kid. He began fiddling with the pot, opening the lid and peering inside. 'I'll ride back to the river and get some water!'

'We don't have any teabags.'

Luke snorted. 'We can use gum leaves!'

Jess grimaced. 'I'm not drinking that.' Then she noticed a collection of small rusty tins sitting on one of the horizontal beams. Most were empty, but one had some fossilised brown stuff caked in the bottom of it. 'Reckon it's coffee?' she asked, handing it to Luke.

He sniffed it. 'Might be.'

Jess picked up another tin. It was enamelled blue, and through the flakes of rust she could just make out a picture of a bird on it. She twisted the top off. Inside was a crackly paper package. 'Tealeaves!' She carefully pulled the package out, prised it open and pressed the crunchy small leaves between her fingers. 'Or something illegal . . .'

Luke peered inside it. 'It's tea, you ninny.'

'No cups.'

'We'll use the empty tins.' Luke took the pot and headed back out into the rain. He straddled Legsy and cantered out of sight.

Jess sat in the doorway of the hut with her feet on the step. The eave was just wide enough to keep the rain off her. She hugged herself, thinking how good a hot drink would be, and looked across the grassy flat.

A small dark head popped up above the grass. And another. Wallabies with beautiful chocolate-brown faces nibbled at the grasses, the rain rolling off their thick fur. The sight of them made Jess relax. Wallabies were always the first to flee if there was danger. The brumby-runners must be long gone.

As though testing her theory, the wallabies suddenly lifted their heads and pricked their ears. Jess peered out along the track and saw Luke approaching on Legsy, the reins in one hand, the pot in the other.

Luke got a fire roaring within minutes, feeding it with big, seasoned logs until the heat of it nearly forced Jess out the door again. He scraped the hot coals into a mound and sat the billy on top. In barely a minute it was bubbling. Luke wrapped his shirt around the handle and poured the boiling water over the tealeaves.

They sat side by side in the doorway, looking out over the grassy flat, sipping on the hot tea.

'This tastes really bad,' said Jess.

Luke picked up the package and read the small print on the back of it. 'It's probably more than fifty years old.' He laughed. 'And it has mouse droppings in it.'

Jess spat hers out but she couldn't help laughing. When she looked up, the breath was knocked from her lungs. 'Look!' she breathed.

A horse, red like ochre, walked onto the grassy flat in the pouring rain. With his scarred, knobbly legs and grey chin, he looked as old and weathered as the granite tors that rose all around him. He let out a long whinny, then walked in circles with his nose high, neighing and calling. Then he stood, silent, with his rump to the wind, and waited.

'Over there,' Luke whispered.

From between two boulders a small coloured mare, with rope burns on her neck and patches of hair missing from her tail, walked slowly, painfully, onto the flat. A foal walked quietly beside her.

The rain beat down on the roof of the hut so hard that it blurred all other sound, but Jess imagined the soft nickering and gentle snorts as the two old horses reunited, ran their noses reassuringly over each other's necks and flanks and pressed their bodies together.

With the small foal gambolling alongside, they walked to the trees and disappeared back into the forest.

Jess ran the back of her hand across her eyes. 'That was so beautiful.'

Luke looked at her with shining eyes. 'That was the horse Mum told me about, Stormy-girl. I'm sure of it.'

21

THE RUNNERS WERE TAKEN to Armidale police station, but Jess, Luke, Grace and Mrs Arnold gave their statements in the pool room at the pub, just as Barker had said. Jess dismissed her ride to the secret valley with Rambo as a dream, a brief period of unconsciousness, as it might well have been.

The place, so exquisitely special, must be kept secret.

Barker rang Jess's parents and the phone was passed around to nearly everyone in the pub before Caroline was swayed from the idea of driving down to retrieve her daughter. Jess could stay one more night, under lock and key with Mrs Arnold, and under the secondary supervision of the local cop.

By late that night they had all made statements and they settled in for a hot meal. Jess tucked in to her roast dinner feeling she could eat half a cow. Beef and roast veg swimming in gravy had never tasted so good.

It turned into an all-night bragging session. Grace launched into a livewire account of galloping over cliff-tops, her stories not unlike an iconic Australian poem, until she noticed Jess's deep frown.

'I told you to be careful with Dodger,' Jess said.

'Well, I was,' said Grace, toning it down. 'I was in perfect control the whole time! Where did you get to, anyway?'

Jess didn't have to answer as Barker and Luke started talking about the dogs.

'Should have called that black dog of yours Satan,' said Barker. 'Make a good guard dog.'

'Yes, well, he is a Mount Isa Runner,' said Grace.

Luke coughed uncomfortably. 'Err, actually, he's a Mount Isa Shepherd.'

'Thought he was a Mount Isa *Sniffer*,' said Barker, looking up from his lasagne.

'All of the above,' said Luke airily. 'Different states call 'em by different names. The breed is only just getting established so there's been some confusion over what to call them. Mostly because they're such a versatile breed, they can do it all, really.'

'Right,' said Barker, sounding very sceptical.

Jess told them about Stormy-girl reuniting with her stallion down on the grassy flat and Grace whined with disappointment at not having been there.

'It'll be hard to prosecute those blokes,' Barker commented when talk returned to the runners.

'Why?' asked Jess. 'It's totally illegal to chase or harass wild horses.'

'Only in national parks. Technically, they were on private land,' said Barker. 'In the eyes of the law, brumbies are pests, like feral pigs or feral goats.'

'But they're not hurting anyone!' said Jess.

'They run over the boundaries into the national parks. There are no fences up there to keep them out. The parks have every right to be concerned about them. They spend a lot of money and resources trying to control brumby numbers. It makes it a lot harder for them when more keep arriving from neighbouring land.'

'So, who *does* own all that land up there?' Jess asked.

'According to the records, the Mathews family,' said Barker. 'They were the original settlers of this area. But when the cattle leases ran out, their station wasn't big enough to be viable. There's still an old hut up there but no one looks after it.' He shrugged. 'The land is about to be seized by the state, and the sooner the better if you ask me. It's become a lawless frontier. Someone needs to manage it properly.'

'But if we could find a descendant, an owner, the brumbies could stay?'

Barker looked at her with a sympathetic face. 'Even if

you did find the owner, what are the chances that they'd want to deal with a load of feral horses? They might want to get rid of them too.'

Jess slept restlessly in the bunkhouse that night. When her back could no longer handle the sagging bed, she dragged the mattress onto the floor and lay quietly with her thoughts. The secret place Luke's mother had spoken about – was it the place that Rambo had taken her to?

Matheson. The name was so similar to Mathews. Could it be possible that they were related? But surely the whole town would know if Luke's family traced back to the original settlers. Was the name Matty's Creek a tribute to Luke's mother, or just a shortened version of Mathews' Creek, like the Matty's Flat Hotel? All these M names – it got to be confusing. These thoughts kept her awake until the morning sunlight began peeking through the slit in the bunkhouse curtains. Jess slipped into her clothes and slunk out the door.

There was a strangeness about this time of day. Some of it was to do with the light, which could barely filter through the thick fog. The carpark was empty, all was quiet and the lights were out in the pub, except for a small bulb over the doorway. Jess sank her hands into the warmth of her pockets and walked towards the road.

The timber bridge, under the cover of the camphor-laurel trees, was still wet with mist and rain. Frogs gurgled and croaked in the river bed like a cart rolling back and forth over rough timber. The water was much deeper than the Coachwood River and the rocks were sharp and blocky.

As Jess crossed the bridge, she thought about how fate had so radically changed Luke's life. A car with a drunk driver, a young mother in the front and her small child in the back. It was such a short drive from the pub. Heck, she and Gracie had done it themselves just a couple of nights ago.

It seemed that the stream could not carry away the sadness that flowed in its waters, that it was picked up by the sound of the wind and carried into the mountains. Was Luke comforted by this place, Jess wondered? Would his coming home calm the troubled spirits of his parents, soothe them and release them?

A small signpost pointed to the cemetery. Jess walked along the bitumen road with mist billowing from her nostrils, nose burning with cold. In the paddocks nearby, horses grazed, silvery shadows in the misty half-light.

The cemetery was a small, square patch cut into a forest of ribbon gums, with long strips of bark hanging in their crowns. The fence rails were thick with soft, fluffy moss and brilliant orange fungi.

Jess slipped through the gate and walked across the neatly kept grass. Early-morning blades of sun cut through the mist, making the marble gravestones twinkle, eerie and surreal. Among them were timber crosses and old lumps of stone, too weathered to carry names any more.

She read the plaques and stones, searching for the name Mathews. Some were quite recent, others were old. Some had shifted with the sinking soil beneath, and stood crooked and wonky.

And then she saw it: a plain marble stone with *MATHESON* etched across the top. Below that were Luke's parents' names. So they were buried together, just as Kitty had said. That was nice, given the long, sad time they had spent apart. On the ground was a small clump of grasses and flowers, roots and soil clinging to the ends, still fresh. From Luke, Jess imagined.

There were no other Mathesons that she could find. She wandered through small clusters of stones, looking for any Mathewses.

She eventually found two small headstones under an old, old blackbutt tree, unremarkable but for their plainness, one rectangular, one rounded, so close that they were touching.

Jess crouched and ran her hand over the scratchy green-blue lichen, feeling for any grooves, carvings, names, but she was unable to make out any letters. She stood back and, from a metre or so away, could make out some letters on each stone. GM on one and LMM on the other. Her eyes caught another stone, too perfectly rounded to be incidental, poking out of the ground. The gravestone of an infant, maybe.

'Who were you?' she whispered to the stones.

The mist seemed to thicken suddenly and the air turned to drizzle. Jess loved the way it felt on her face – so soft and gentle. But soon it began to soak into her clothes. She walked back to the road and continued towards Matty's Creek.

The drizzle stopped as quickly as it had come, and sunlight slipped through the clouds in little streams of gold. Jess enjoyed the soft sun on her face and the crispness of the breeze that pushed the clouds from the sky and freshened and dried the valley around her. As her circulation improved, she took off her jacket and tied it around her waist, letting the early winter sun warm her arms.

At the property, Filth limped towards her, tail wagging feebly. Both his front legs had squares shaved off them, and most of his neck had been shaved too, revealing a big, colourful swelling.

'Filthy.' Jess sank to her knees and wrapped her arms gently around the big dog's body. He whined and wiggled in appreciation. 'You're okay.' He smelled better than usual, too. 'Did somebody wash you?' She gave him a scratch behind the ears. 'Where's your master, hey?'

She went to look for Luke, and found him floating in the river behind the dilapidated house, wearing a pair of old work shorts. His torso was white against his singlet-tanned shoulders and arms, which fanned slowly back and forth in the icy water.

'Aren't you frozen?'

He lifted his head, seeming unsurprised. 'Come in, it's really nice.'

'No way.' She pointed up to the mountain behind them. 'It snowed up there yesterday!'

'It hasn't melted yet. The river's still warm from summer.' Luke pushed a wave of water at her and she squealed and jumped back. 'You know I'll drag you in,' he warned.

He would, she knew he would. He always did, chasing her across the river flats till he caught her and dragged her, kicking and screaming, into the Coachwood River, usually fully clothed.

Seeing as she was wearing the only clothes she had to wear home, Jess conceded. Luke watched her strip off to her undies and tank top and wade in, gasping as the cold rushed up her legs and took her breath away. He took her by the hand and unceremoniously yanked her into the water with him, making her scream.

She threw her arms around his neck and wrapped her

legs around his hips, trying to pull herself up out of the icy water. 'It's f-f-f-*freezing*!'

He tightened his arms around her waist and pulled her downwards, submerging her completely. She came up gasping again with her hair washed back over her head, her face icy and cleansed and stinging with blood and life. Her shoulders prickled with goosebumps and she reached down and pressed her lips to his, kissing warmth into her soul.

He kissed around her ears, down her neck and across her cheek. Then his lips were on hers and he was pulling her close. She wrapped her arms around his neck and kissed him back, and the whole time, the terrifying thought that it might be her last ever kiss with him made her hold him even harder.

'What's wrong?' he whispered, pulling away and searching her face.

'You're going to stay here, aren't you? You're not coming home.' She searched his face, but there was no smile on his face, no laughter in his eyes. The silence was sharp, as though sky and earth had stopped to watch them.

Jess tried to smile but she could feel it come out all twisted. She drew a long, steadying breath.

Luke held her face in both hands and wiped the tears off her cheeks with his thumbs. He kissed around her eyes. 'Oh God, please don't cry,' he whispered.

'I can't help it,' she whispered back.

He kissed her and the love and sadness held in his kisses only made her heart rip more. For the first time since she had known him, she felt as though she was losing him, to the one thing that might hold more power over him, something she knew he yearned for deeply, and that was family, blood relatives and a sense of belonging.

'Shhhh,' Luke whispered softly in her ear.

'Sorry,' she sniffed back.

'No. Shhhh,' he whispered again.

She pulled away and saw Luke's finger pressed to his lips. His gaze was directed over her shoulder. He slowly moved around and held her where she could look down the river, and she froze with wonder.

At a small glade, three horses drank together from the edge of the river, sucking the cool water through their teeth and letting it lap over their nostrils. Jess barely dared to breathe as two more, a dull chestnut and a dark bay, approached from behind and joined them.

A gust of wind rustled over the trees and all at once the horses became nervous, lifting their heads and sniffing, testing the scents that travelled on the breeze. In a sudden explosion of movement, tumbling rocks and snapping branches, they crashed through the forest, hooves cracking on the rocks, thundering back up the hillside until they disappeared.

Jess smiled at Luke. He belonged to this river and these mountains. Just as the brumbies ran through the trees and the river cut through the valley, the horses and the land cut through his heart. They wove in and out of him like threads of gold through beautiful white river quartz. 'Will you come and visit us?'

'Don't talk like that.'

She ran her finger over the moonstone hanging in the hollow of his throat, and when he reached to untie it she put her hand over his and stopped him. 'You keep it. I don't want a stone. I want you.'

'I just need a bit more time down here,' he said.

'How much time?'

'Just a few weeks, until the next holidays. Then I'll come home.'

'What about Sapphire's mares?'

He looked at her with soft brown eyes.

'You want me to look after them?' she asked.

'Just until the holidays. If it's a hassle, I'm sure Corey would . . .'

'No, no,' she said. 'I don't mind. I'll enjoy it.' She kissed him again. 'Just a few weeks. Promise?'

'Moonstone promise.'

22

LATE ON TUESDAY NIGHT, Jess sat cross-legged on her bed at home and let the cool southerly breeze drift in through the window. Outside, she could see the Southern Cross dangling against a clear black sky. Dodger looked up from under the giant tree in the front paddock, snorted, and got back to grazing.

'How are the brumbies?' Jess's dad had asked when Mrs Arnold dropped her home, without looking up from the telly.

'Great, we managed to rescue some,' she said, lugging her duffle bag off her shoulder and plonking it outside the laundry with a thud. She told him about the creamy filly with blue eyes. 'We called her Min Min.'

'How's Luke?' Craig asked.

'I think we re-homed him, too.' After that, Jess had gone straight to her room and flopped on her bed.

She lay back now, looking up at the timber ceiling,

painted in a creamy white. The soft green walls around her were almost entirely covered with ribbons and sashes and photos of horses. There were school awards, too. Plenty of them. Shara was right. She didn't want to dunce out and not finish school.

She would live her life and let Luke sort out his own. It would take more than a mountain to come between her and Luke. Surely he'd meant it when he said he would come back to Coachwood Crossing.

Jess closed her eyes and surrendered to the exhaustion she felt. She gave only a mumbled 'goodnight' when her mum came in, and was grateful to feel her boots being pulled from her feet. She barely noticed the doona being tossed over her and tucked in around her chin, or the light on her bedside table being snapped off. She slept.

And in the middle of the night, when her phone buzzed in the depths of her duffle bag full of damp clothes, she wasn't sure if she was dreaming or not.

The next day it seemed nearly impossible for Jess to drag herself out of bed and haul on her school uniform.

'Working with Luke this arvo?' asked her dad as he sat down to a bowl of cereal.

'He's still down south,' said Jess. She gave him a quick update on Luke's new life.

Caroline joined Craig at the kitchen bench. 'What's he going to do with all his brumbies?'

'Lawson's have all been sold to a trainer. He found someone who wanted horses for riding clinics. I'll still help Luke train and re-home his.'

'And now he's taken off again?' Caroline looked livid.

'Knew he would,' said Craig.

Had he taken off? Jess didn't know if he had or not. She hadn't had time to process it yet. But she knew that a heavy ache, a numbness, was building in her chest and she was doing her best to ignore it. Luke had gone away before, but he had always come back. This time, she wasn't so sure he would.

'Oh well, a woman's destiny must be her own,' said Jess. 'Now, I have to get ready for school.' She left her parents staring dumbstruck at each other.

She stumbled out the door and down the front steps, shoving her riding jeans into her schoolbag. She threw hay to the horses and walked hurriedly to the school bus, realising too late that she had left both her lunch and her phone behind.

She found an old brekkie bar in the pocket of her bag and a bruised green pear, and made that her breakfast. She combed her hair as she watched the paddocks and hills roll past. The bus picked up more kids in town and she rummaged around in her bag to find her diary, which might give her some clue as to what was expected of her that day.

Wednesday went slowly. Jess drifted through the day like early morning fog over the mountain cemetery. It was difficult to get back into the groove of classes, libraries, books and smartboards.

She tried not to think of Luke, swimming in the freezing river and riding through the mountains, snow whirling around him. She wanted to message him and find out how Filth was going, but her phone was at home. He wouldn't get her calls anyway, unless he was up a tree for some reason.

Jess used her lunch break to belt through some homework so she could go and see Luke's brumbies after school. She was dying to see Opal too. She wondered all day if the traumatised horses were any more settled, or if they had gone the way of their stallion.

When she got to Harry's she found Luke's wildies looking healthier – their flanks had filled out and their various wounds seemed to be healing. But they were as jittery as ever, starting at the slightest noise and staying closely huddled together. The sight of them filled her head with images of nets and trucks and boat winches.

Jess held a carrot through the fence to Opal. 'Hey,

girl.' She smiled as she ran her hands over the filly's neck. 'I missed you.' She glanced at the brumby mares behind as Opal took the entire carrot and crunched on it whole. 'Fancy not knowing the joys of root vegetables.'

Rosie and Corey arrived on their horses.

'How have you gone with these guys?' asked Jess, glancing at the brumbies.

'Still can't get anywhere near them,' said Corey. 'I've tried a few times and they just totally freak out.'

'How about Lawson's ones?'

Corey's face brightened. 'They're going great. John gelded the two colts and I've taught them to lead.'

He bent down from his saddle and opened the gate to the arena, where Lawson's six wild horses chewed on hay. He ushered one of the geldings out into the arena and began riding around behind it. Jess watched in amazement as he pushed his horse into a canter and began circling around the trotting brumby at a slow lope, gradually getting closer. When he got alongside, he leaned over and slipped a halter over the brumby's ears. It shook its head but kept trotting. Corey let it run and kept circling it around and around, without putting any pressure on the rope.

After a minute or so, the brumby settled into a rhythm and Corey kept cantering, circling, circling, then reached down and gently ran a hand over the gelding's back and neck, then over its rump. Jess was surprised at how accepting the animal was. Corey looped a rope around the horse's rump and encouraged it to walk up alongside his horse. He led it for a couple of circles each way, asked it to stop and then removed the rope and halter and let the brumby go. It whinnied and trotted back to its mob.

Jess opened the gate with a smile on her face. She had to admit that was skilful riding, and great horsemanship.

'It's a cool technique, isn't it?' said Rosie, still sitting on Buster and watching from the sidelines.

'Sure is,' Jess agreed. 'They're ready to go to their new home.'

'Have a turn,' offered Corey. 'Try the other gelding.'

Jess spent the afternoon on Dodger, with Rosie and Corey on the rails instructing her, haltering the brumbies one by one, circling, running her hands over them and then releasing them.

'You guys have done such an amazing job,' said Jess, as she let the last one go. But she couldn't help feeling sad about Luke's mob of three wildies. Would they ever adapt to their new surroundings?

The next day, Jess woke feeling desperately blank. She hunted for her phone, but in vain. The emptiness of being apart from Luke stayed with her all day. It couldn't be healthy, she thought, to miss someone so much, to be so miserable without them.

'A woman's destiny must be her own,' she scrawled absent-mindedly across the inside of her textbook. But she was having trouble believing it.

23

JESS SAT IN CLASS, willing herself to keep it together until she got to Harry's. Being with the horses would make everything better. She needed to be near them, to see the calmness in Dodger's eyes, be mesmerised by Opal's easy lope.

That afternoon, she helped Corey and Rosie with the trapped brumbies again. This time they were able to lead all of them around off the side of their horses. Jess spent some time with each one, off the back of Dodger, teaching them how to 'follow a feel' and give to the gentle pressure of the ropes, how to step into the release and come willingly forward. They quickly became light and responsive. It was fantastic progress and soon she became lost in their world again.

As she helped feed up that night, Jess felt certain that all of Lawson's brumbies would make good riding mounts. But the same couldn't be said for Sapphire's mares. Jess walked to their yard and found them eating hay with Opal. They jumped when they saw her and began milling around nervously, trying to hide between each other, packing into a tight group. Jess took a rope and walked into the yard. She would take Opal home tonight. Dodger was too lonely without her. He had whinnied all night.

Opal stood slightly to the outside of the mares. Surely it wouldn't upset them too much if she just nicked into the yard and led Opal out of there. Jess made a loop with the rope and coiled it in her hand as she approached the filly, then fumbled it and dropped one end. She stooped to pick it up.

Without warning, Opal's shoulder barged into her, sending her sprawling into the mud. She saw hooves and legs coming at her and rolled quickly away and under the fence.

Rosie ran to her. 'You okay?'

Jess clutched her throbbing shoulder and winced. 'Landed on my arm,' she groaned.

In the yard the mare swung her rump around and lifted her tail, squirting and winking.

'They're horsing like mad,' said Rosie. 'It's sending Biyanga nuts. We had to lock him in his stable.'

Jess stood in the gateway and called Opal over, waiting until the brumby mares were at the other side of the yard before letting Opal out. She watched them as she closed the gate.

'We'll have to do something with them soon. They can't stay in here the rest of their lives,' said Rosie from behind her. 'Luke needs to come back.'

As Jess settled into bed that night, she heard a muffled ring. She lifted her head and listened. Her phone! Where *was* it?

She leapt out of bed and flew to the laundry, diving on her duffle bag and madly excavating. Nothing. She stopped. Listened. Saw a faint glow down the side of the washing machine. How the heck had it got under there? It was lit up and vibrating and she pounced on it, slamming her finger onto the button and pressing it to her ear, hoping like mad it hadn't rung out.

'Yes?'

'Jess!'

'Luke?'

She heard him sigh with relief. 'Jessy.'

'It's nearly midnight, you mad thing,' she whispered, unable to contain her happiness.

'I'm sitting on Rambo. It's a full moon. I'm on top of

the mountain and there is snow everywhere. It's amazing, Jessy!'

'Wow.' She wished desperately she was there, on the back of Rambo with him.

'The little creamy foal, the one you saved. It's back with its mum!'

'Min Min,' said Jess. 'We called her Min Min.'

'I've been trying to ring you and tell you.'

'I lost my phone.' She didn't think he could get coverage, except from . . .

'I miss you, Jess.'

'I miss you too.'

'Yeah, but I miss you *heaps*.'

'Is it keeping you awake at night?'

'Yeah.'

'Thought it might be.' Jess laughed as she crept back to her bedroom and crawled under the covers. A smile spread over her face as she lay back against her pillow. 'Am I having a dream or something?'

'Depends. Are you dreaming about me?'

'I always dream about you.'

'I would dream about you too if I could get to sleep in the first place.'

'You need a therapy pet.'

Before she could tell him about Sapphire's mares, the phone went dead. 'Luke? You there?'

It had lost reception. She lay with the phone held against her chest, bitterly disappointed, hoping it would ring again.

So this was what their relationship would be: broken phone calls in the middle of the night, whenever he had the energy to go up the mountain. She finally gave up and willed herself to sleep. If it was all she could have of him, she would take it.

24

LAWSON'S BRUMBIES PROGRESSED quickly. Once they could lead and tie up, load on and off a horse float, graze inside a fenced paddock and pick up all their feet without fuss, Lawson called the buyer and told him the horses were ready.

A man arrived one afternoon in a small horse truck. While Lawson talked to him, Jess slipped a halter around Buddy and led him to the loading ramp. 'You be good,' she said, letting the little pale chestnut nuzzle at her hands. 'You show them what fine horses the tablelands brumbies are.'

She slung the rope over his neck, turned his head towards the opening of the truck and slapped him on the rump. 'Walk up,' she said, letting him load himself.

Buddy scrambled quickly up the ramp and walked into the back of the truck. He turned his hindquarters so that he stood alongside the partitions. Jess followed and closed the steel divider beside him, making way for the next horse. Then she tied his halter to the bars on the small window. 'You have a fun life, Buddy,' she said, giving him a final pat goodbye.

Corey led the next horse up, and one by one, all six of Lawson's brumbies were loaded and tethered securely inside the truck. Jess took a last look at them and felt an enormous sense of satisfaction. They were beautiful horses, kind by nature, hardy and athletic.

She cast her mind back to the first day she had met Luke, loping around an arena on a fine black colt he had broken in himself, a mixed-up kid full of aggro and confusion. These brumbies would soon sort out another bunch of mixed-up kids at Lawson's friend's clinic.

They know everything you're thinking. They just mirror what you do.

Lawson joined her at the fence as the truck pulled out of the driveway and rolled down the road. 'Hear from Luke yet?'

'Yeah, only for a minute, then the phone cut out,' said Jess. 'There's no reception down there.'

'Tell me about it,' said Lawson, sounding annoyed. 'What's he doing, is he coming back?'

Jess shrugged. 'He told me he'd be back by next school holidays.'

'He said the same to me,' said Lawson. 'But I just got a

call from TAFE. He's been making enquiries about trans-
ferring his farrier's apprenticeship to a college down there.'

Jess looked at Lawson with her mouth open.

'He didn't tell you either, did he?' Lawson looked
unimpressed. 'Sorry to bring bad news, kid.' He turned
and walked back to the house.

Jess stood alone, staring up the road. She could still
hear the fading engine of the horse truck, grinding its
gears as it made its way around the bends in the road.

Jess sat under the big coachwood tree, staring gloomily
through the fence rails at Luke's miserable-looking brumbies. The foal was a sooty dun, or buckskin. There was
nothing pretty about him — he looked as though he had
been rolled in dirt — but he was a nice enough type and
would probably make a good station horse.

'Maybe we should wean that colt,' said Corey, sitting
beside her. 'Must be a yearling. Be impossible to handle
him with his mad mother nearby.'

'And what about the two mares?'

'Bush 'em somewhere. We'll never get them broke.
They're too old, too wild.'

'Blakely Downs.'

'Or down at Luke's place.'

'You mean *Matty's Creek*,' said Jess. She glared at Corey. '*This* is Luke's place, *here*.'

Corey looked slightly bewildered. 'Whatever . . . Has he put in any fences yet?'

'How would I know?' said Jess. 'He doesn't tell me anything. I can't even reach him on the phone.'

'Let's get the poor things into a paddock. Then at least they can eat some grass,' he said. 'Come on, I'll help you.'

Jess and Corey spent what was left of the day setting up a brumby paddock for Sapphire's mares. They chose one with lots of trees and checked over all the electric wiring. Finally, Jess and Opal led them out of the yard and down the laneway. They followed warily, eyes rolling all over the place. Once inside the paddock, Jess led Opal around the fenced boundary and then took her to the trough for a drink. Finally, she unbuckled the filly's halter and released her with the mares.

'Look, they're grazing already,' said Corey. 'Bet that tastes good.'

The chestnut mare ran her nose along the ground and took mouthfuls of grass. The bay and her foal followed.

'I just hope they don't gallop through the fences.'

'They've had a good look at them,' said Corey. 'One zap and they'll soon learn they can't go through them.'

Jess watched them a while longer before feeling satisfied they wouldn't hurt themselves. Back at the stables,

Dodger was still saddled. Jess vaulted onto him, then took Opal's rope and led her alongside.

As she rode out the gate, Jess turned back to Corey. 'I'll try and get a message to Luke. See what he wants to do with them.'

Corey nodded and closed the gate for her.

She rode home along the river flats in the dark, crossing creeks and brushing through the long grass. She took a long detour up to Mossy Mountain and Dodger picked his way over the windy trail as though it were broad daylight. Jess marvelled at how well horses could see at night.

At the top, she looked out over the valley at the sparsely scattered lights of the farm houses. A cool southerly caressed her face. She pulled her phone from her saddlebags and sent a text message to Luke.

I think you should come and get the brumby mares.

25

JESS WAITED ON HER front verandah with her duffle bag stuffed full and her swag rolled up. Nerves flitted about in her stomach. God, how many times had she felt like this?

Lawson's truck finally swung into her driveway. It stopped by the house, motor running.

She'd only had two other phone calls from Luke over the past three weeks. Both times they had been cut short. Nothing was said about colleges and there was no mention of him staying or leaving. The subject was left dangling in the air, unacknowledged.

Which was good, she told herself. It allowed her to concentrate on school and get really good marks. She came home triumphantly with her exam results, knowing they would give her strong leverage should she need to negotiate holidays with her parents. Craig and Caroline agreed to let her go back to Mathews' Flat, to help resettle the brumby mares.

When Luke jumped out of the truck, there was no big swirling hug. Just a quick, awkward embrace. 'Hey,' he said.

'Hey,' she said back.

Grace's head poked out the window. 'Hurry up and get in, Jessy. We gotta make dinner time at the Matty's Flat Hotel!'

The thought of Kitty's roast dinner made Jess's spirits lift a little.

Luke took her swag and swung it up into the back of the truck through a small side door. She pushed her duffle bag in after it and, through a gap in the side boards, she saw the hooves of the brumby mares.

'Are you going to let them go?' she asked.

'It's private land,' said Luke. 'No one can stop me.'

Jess climbed up next to Grace.

Luke barely had time to close the door before Lawson rolled back down the driveway. From the packing shed, Craig waved and Jess watched in the truck's side mirror as the house disappeared behind her.

Hours later, the truck's engine groaned as it climbed ever upward into the tablelands country. The headlights made a tunnel of grey and soft blue before them.

Light bounced off the silvery uprights of gum trees, and reflectors lit the side of the road like fairy lights. On the back the two mares and the yearling foal clattered about as they tried to keep their footing.

When they pulled to a stop outside the Matty's Flat Hotel it was nine-thirty and all Jess could think about was roast beef and veggies swimming in Kitty's homemade gravy.

She helped Luke check the horses before dinner. They spread out straw, lugged buckets of water and broke open a bale of hay. The mares began eating immediately.

'They look happier than they did this afternoon,' said Luke, sounding surprised. 'More content. Maybe they like the truck or something.' He shrugged. 'Or maybe they're just tired.'

'Maybe they know they're going home,' said Jess, as she watched the tired buckskin foal nuzzle down into a bed of straw. 'They can smell the mountains.'

'I can't wait to release them in the morning,' said Luke, 'and watch them gallop back into the wild.'

'Same.'

Inside the pub, the fire was roaring around a huge stack of sawn logs. Barker and Steve were standing by the fireplace and Kitty was behind the bar. Luke made a big deal of introducing Lawson as his brother, and much hand-shaking and jocularity followed. They'd barely had time to get a drink when Rosie and Mrs Arnold walked in, followed by Tom and Corey.

For a moment, Jess felt she had been transported back to Coachwood Crossing. 'There's only one person missing,' she said.

'No, there's not,' grinned Corey.

Jess felt two slim hands wrap over her eyes. She would know them anywhere. 'Sharsy!' She spun around to find her bestie grinning at her. 'How did *you* get here?' she squeaked.

'Canningdale is only an hour's drive away. Corey picked me up,' said Shara. 'I heard there was a big house-warming party on, and a brumby release!'

'I can't wait to see those mares gallop back into the mountain,' said Grace excitedly. 'There was no *way* I was going to miss that.'

They ordered meals and pushed several tables together, rearranging the tiny pub lounge until it resembled a private function room. Barker joined them and, as the meals were the last ones to be served in the pub for the night, so did Kitty and Steve.

Kitty shared more memories of her friendship with Matilda, or Matty, as she called her. Their times together sounded so much like the adventures Jess had shared with her girlfriends: long trail rides and cattle drives, brumby-spotting and birthing foals. Luke listened quietly and intently.

Jess watched her three best girlfriends, all laughing around the table together in their riding jeans and woolly jumpers. She couldn't begin to imagine what it would be like to ever lose one of them as Kitty had lost Matty.

Kitty told Luke about his parents' wedding, at the small timber church with the four square windows. They hadn't been able to squeeze everyone in. She told them how Matilda had met Jack, a logger from Dorrigo, in this very pub. After that, Jack came back every Friday night to see the band that used to play in the beer garden and Matilda would turn herself inside out trying to find the right dress to wear. 'She was so crazy about this Jack fella.'

He was a charmer, a larrikin, and would dance Matilda from one end of the beer garden to the other, nearly knocking people's plates from their tables, and upsetting the old cockies who had come for a quiet beer.

The forty hectares on the river was their wedding present from Matilda's parents, who cut it off their own land. 'Cut off the bit with the crappy old house on it and went and built a nice new one for themselves,' said Kitty.

'So Jack Ernest Matheson was never a local,' said Jess. 'He was a blow-in.'

'That's right,' said Kitty. 'It was Matty's family who were the locals, not Jack's.'

Jess sighed. There went her theory of the name Matheson somehow being linked to the original settlers of this mountain range.

The subject came back around to the brumbies and the wild horses. Rambo was a wedding gift from Matty to Jack. She had trapped him as a yearling colt with salt and lucerne at the back of her parents' property. They had broken him in together, as well as several others.

'They loved riding through those mountains,' said Kitty. 'They would disappear nearly every weekend. Matty used to tell stories, about secret glades and special places. She wanted to write books about them.'

'I remember her stories,' said Luke. 'You used to read them to me.'

Kitty looked delighted. 'You remember!'

'It's like being in a storybook when you're up there,' agreed Jess. 'It's so beautiful.'

'Especially when it snows,' said Grace.

'You were lucky to see that,' said Steve. 'It doesn't snow up there every year.'

'Here's to the brumbies,' said Mrs Arnold, raising a schooner of port, 'and their little part of the world. May they run free for years to come.'

Jess noticed that Barker was the only one not to raise

his glass. She looked at him questioningly.

'What's up, Barky?' said Steve, still jovial.

The sergeant exhaled and his face seemed grim. He looked around at all of them, as though he was about to deliver bad news.

'What?' said Kitty, smiling.

'They won't be up there for years to come. Haven't you heard?' he said in a quiet voice.

'Heard what?'

'The council have put out public notices. If that land's not claimed by next month, the brumbies will be culled and the land will be auctioned off.'

Everyone looked at Barker, aghast. 'Hey?'

He gave a helpless shrug. 'There's more than five thousand hectares of unclaimed private title up there. It's been vacant for nearly fifty years. Everyone wants a piece of it. The national parks want the feral horses culled and the land returned to wilderness. The forestry department wants to log it. The police want to stop all the illegal shooting that goes on up there. The farmers all want to see it subdivided and turned into grazing properties. It's such fertile country and it's being taken over by feral horses, rednecks and weeds.'

Barker looked from face to face and shook his head. 'I'm sorry, but the days of those wild horses up there are seriously numbered.'

Everyone at the table stopped talking and the celebratory atmosphere took a sharp dive. Mrs Arnold muttered something profoundly rude.

Jess's thoughts went immediately to the small pond at the bottom of the big granite cliffs. The place, on the tablelands, where the boundaries met. She had seen it with her own eyes. The unclaimed place, where Saladin's spirit was born to the blue-eyed brumbies . . .

The place, so exquisitely special . . .

It was about to be destroyed.

Later that night, Jess found Luke outside in the cabin of the truck. On the back, the brumbies munched noisily. 'Hey,' she said softly.

'Hey,' he said, and held out a hand to her.

She climbed up and sat on the bench seat next to him. 'We can't just let them shoot all the brumbies and auction off their home like that.'

'I don't know how we can stop them,' said Luke. 'I can't take on that many horses, Jess. I can't save them all. There are too many of them up there. What would I do with them? I don't even know what to do with these mares on the back now.'

'You have forty hectares.'

'But how would I keep them in? The fences on my place are so old they've nearly all fallen over.'

Jess was quiet for a while, and they both sat there, adrift in their own thoughts.

'The secret place, the one your mum talked about. I've seen it,' she finally whispered. 'Rambo took me there. It's a foaling place.'

'I know.' Luke nodded solemnly. 'I've seen it too.'

Kitty fussed around in the bunkhouse, billowing fresh white sheets over the beds. 'Wasn't expecting so many of you,' she chirped.

Jess took the other side of the sheet and helped her tuck it in.

'Some sneaky backpacker stole one of my chenille bedspreads,' Kitty said, as she ripped a brand-new quilt from its packaging. 'It was nearly fifty years old, retro.' She looked suspiciously at Mrs Arnold.

'Probably time to replace them anyway,' mumbled Mrs Arnold, shooting a threatening look at Jess and Grace.

The thick padded quilt was a welcome upgrade from the flimsy chenille, but Jess's thoughts were not so comfortable. In only a few weeks Brumby Mountain would be auctioned off. The unclaimed pocket of land with the breakaway herd of brumbies would be claimed. And, most likely, the horses would be trapped, shot, or run off the land.

'How could so much land just be forgotten?' she wondered out loud. 'Has anyone even tried to track down the original Mathews family?'

'Why would they?' said Mrs Arnold, as she pulled the quilt over her shoulders and snapped off the light.

Jess lay in the darkness, trying to put the pieces of Luke's history together. She couldn't let go of the idea that, somehow, he was connected to that land and the horses up there. But she couldn't quite work out how.

26

THE NEXT MORNING the sound of a chainsaw echoed off the granite cliffs surrounding Matty's Creek. Jess found Luke and Lawson splitting posts to make a yard for the brumby mares. Steve was on a tractor with a post-hole digger on the back groaning and spiralling into the ground.

The truck, with the brumbies on board, was parked by the river under the shade of the trees. Jess heard them whinnying in the back. A soft, brown nose appeared at one of the upper windows.

Luke pulled off his earmuffs and dropped his axe when he saw Jess. He waved her into the shed, away from the noise of the chainsaw. 'They know they're home,' he said. 'They haven't stopped calling since we got here. There are horses up in the hills calling back.'

'Are you going to let them go?'

'No, not yet,' said Luke. 'Not until I know they won't be shot.'

Jess noticed that the shed had been cleared out. The boys' swags were rolled out on the raised boards of the mezzanine floor. Below, on the ground, was a table, chairs and an old forty-four-gallon drum that had been cut to make a wood stove.

'Home sweet home, hey?' she said.

Luke nodded. 'For the moment; till I get the rats and snakes out of the house.'

'Are you going to restore it?'

'Don't know if it's worth it. Steve's gonna have a look at it with me later. It's all patched up with fibro and asbestos. It was pretty shonky to begin with.'

'Least it's got a toilet,' said Jess.

Luke laughed. 'The bowl's cracked.' He shrugged. 'But the plumbing still works.'

'Did you have another look through it?' she asked. 'To see if there was anything from your parents worth keeping?'

'Yeah, I found a few old things, but I think locals and vandals got to it before me.' He pointed to a collection of old tins and cups, some enamel plates and bone-handled cutlery on the table.

Jess picked up one of the tins. It was a small tea canister, enamelled blue with a picture on it. 'It's like the one in the hut,' she said. 'Look, it's got a picture of a little bird on it.'

'I didn't notice,' said Luke, stepping closer and peering over her shoulder.

Jess set it back on the table. 'Makes me wonder who put the tea in the hut,' she said, creasing her brow.

'Dunno, but I have to get these yards built,' Luke said suddenly. 'I can't keep these brumbies stuck in the back of the truck. And if the land gets sold, I'll have to fence this place off from the mountain. The brumbies won't be able to come and go any more.'

'You could put a gate in,' Jess suggested.

'Yeah, but I don't know what to do with Rambo,' said Luke. 'I don't know whether to let him out or lock him in.'

That was a tricky one. Suddenly she shared Luke's sense of urgency. 'He's better off in here if all his friends are going to get shot anyway.' Then she shuddered. What a horrible thing to say.

Luke looked grim as he began splitting posts again.

Jess wandered over to the house. Holding her jumper up over her nose, she pulled the old flyscreen open, then pushed at the broken door and scraped it across the floor.

Inside, there was a doorway to her left, another to her right, and the tiny kitchen at the end. A quick glance revealed that the rooms were a mess of upside-down bedsprings and old chaff bags filled with rubbish, broken bottles and graffiti. Someone had already gone through all the stuff. Panels of fibro sheeting hung from the ceiling and up in the roof cavity she could see beams of wood and corrugated iron. A rat scooted across one of the beams and she squirmed.

Luke had taken the table and chairs from the kitchen, and the two cupboard doors below the sink swung open. Yellowed newspaper, an old can of flyspray, rusty steel wool and an old dishwashing brush lay among scattered rat droppings. Gingham curtains hung from a small window, limp and faded.

The fireplace, Jess noticed, was made of stone: rugged pieces stacked and stuck together with some sort of concretey stuff, just like the hut by the river. She banged her fist on the wall and heard no echo. Something very solid was behind the fibro sheets. She pulled at a broken bit and saw slabs of raw-cut timber behind the wall.

It *was* an old hut, just like the one by the river, covered with modern materials and turned into a kitchen. Jess looked at the floor and noticed it was made from hardwood rather than the ply sheeting used in the rest of the small shack. The other two rooms must have been added on.

Jess walked back into the hall and squeezed herself into the first room, pushing sacks stuffed with more sacks – used feedbags, maybe – away with her leg. They were frayed with mouse holes. Beyond them she could see an old glass-doored dresser, filled with books and papers and ornaments. The glass was broken and the clutter spilled out onto the floor.

She sat on the edge of a dusty couch and brushed shards of glass off the papers. They were mostly old vinyl record covers, more newspapers and a handwritten shopping list. Matilda's handwriting, maybe? Jess folded it and put it in her pocket for Luke. Was there any more of her writing, Jess wondered, as she began searching through the old TV remotes, tubes of hand cream and other stuff. She pulled it all out of the dresser but, judging by the way it came out, so random and disorganised, she guessed someone had been through it before her.

She searched beneath and behind the dresser, and rummaged through more junk under the couch and between the old sacks, but found nothing.

In the other room she found more mess, empty beer bottles and cigarette butts strewn across the floor. Picture hooks hung empty on the walls, and cut wires hung from the ceiling where the light fitting had been removed. As Luke had said, anything of any value was long gone, most likely pilfered by local kids.

She leaned against the doorway and tried to imagine Matilda and Jack living here with a two-year-old Luke, riding their brumbies through the mountains and coming home to a small shack at night. Then she thought of the accident that had separated them all. She suddenly understood why a man as lively as Jack had chosen to live alone, where he didn't have to face other people, see his own pain and guilt mirrored in their faces.

As Jess stood propped in the doorway, absorbed in the tragedy of it all, the beam under her hand shifted and there was a creak above her head. She looked up and saw two large sheets of ceiling plaster part, then split down the middle. A beam slid across her field of vision. With startling clarity, she realised the house was collapsing around her.

She bolted for the front door, only two steps away. All around her, the house moved – slowly at first, and then, as she burst out of the door into the open, it crumpled. In a storm of dust and fibro and timber beams, the front of the house came crashing to the ground. The noise was tremendous. In the nearby paddock, kangaroos leapt off the ground and fled for the cover of the trees. Luke, Lawson and Steve looked up from their work in shock.

The dust was unbelievable, full of plaster and rat poo and old cigarette ash, billowing with the residue of other peoples' lives. Jess staggered backwards as it swelled and rolled towards her. She coughed as it entered her lungs.

Luke slowly, disbelievingly, took the earmuffs from

his head again and walked over. He looked at the crumpled mess, then back to Jess, and gave a short, bewildered laugh. 'What happened?'

'Umm, the house fell down.'

He gave her a comical accusing stare. 'No need to wreck the joint.'

'Sorry.'

There was a loud creak and a second crash as the roof collapsed further into the rubble.

Jess and Luke jumped back.

Lawson and Steve appeared alongside them, followed by Grace and Mrs Arnold. They stood staring, dumbstruck, at the sheets of roofing and building rubble. As the dust cleared, a small wood slab hut was revealed, standing there as though the last seventy years had just been peeled off, and they were transported back to another time.

27

THE BOYS WORKED ON the yards until lunchtime, cutting and shaping long branches and wiring them to tree trunks. Luke and Lawson put in new posts where there were no trees, and unbolted the gate from the old sheep yards and hung it off a new corner post that Steve had tamped into the ground with a spud bar. When there was only a small section of railing left to build, they stopped for a break.

'Won't be much longer, girls,' said Luke.

'Still thinking about renovating?' asked Mrs Arnold as she sat on the edge of the river eating pies from the local bakery.

Luke looked forlornly at what was left of the house. 'Might salvage the bathtub,' he said. 'Make a good horse trough.'

'The original hut is cute,' said Jess. 'It must be really old. It's like the one we found in the mountains that time.'

Luke nodded. 'Have to burn the rest, though. It's crawling with termites.'

'Let's have a bonfire tonight,' said Grace cheerfully. 'We'll all sleep out in our swags!'

Jess looked hopefully at Mrs Arnold. She nodded. 'Fine by me. Sounds fun.'

They spent the afternoon on the snigging chain, behind the tractor, dragging all the timber from the house and stacking it into a huge teepee. Jess raked up piles of debris and tossed all the old sacks of rubbish on top. The corrugated iron was stacked by the shed and the old nails collected in a bucket.

It was when Lawson looped the snigging chain around a large section of wall and the tractor started pulling that Jess saw it: a flash of metal glinting in the sunlight, between the timber studs and noggings of the walls.

'Stop!' she yelled, waving her arms at Steve, who was driving the tractor. 'Stop! There's something in there.'

Luke saw it too and began pulling the scraps of splintered timber and broken plasterboard away from the frame. He put his hands into the cavity and jimmied out a large, rectangular tin, the kind Jess's grandmother would have put a Christmas cake in.

He prised open the lid, which had nearly rusted closed. It was stuffed full of papers, old and crumbly. Luke carefully pulled them out and laid them on the grass beside him. Beneath them was a small bundle of pound notes, and rattling in the bottom were two rings and a golden necklace.

'Someone's life savings,' said Mrs Arnold, mesmerised, 'and I bet those are wedding rings.'

'D'you mind?' Jess knelt beside Luke and picked up the rings. They were plain and flat and made from gold, one smaller than the other. She held them in her hand and wondered about their origins.

And then she saw a small, tarnished white box, small enough to fit in the palm of her hand. On the lid, written in old-fashioned typewriter font, it read:

```
            AIF Military Medal
        Awarded to Pte. Gordon Robertson
    For his gallantry and devotion during
            the taking of Beersheba
              31st October 1917
```

'Oh wow, a war medal,' said Jess, carefully pulling the lid off the box. Inside, resting on tissue paper, was a round silver medal, not much larger than a twenty-cent piece. Jess picked it up and turned it carefully around in her hand. A king's head was on the front, and on the back the words FOR BRAVERY IN THE FIELD were inscribed. It hung on a short striped ribbon.

'Where's Beersheba?' asked Luke, leaning over her shoulder.

'It's in Israel,' said Mrs Arnold. 'It's where the Light Horse charged and helped the Allies win the First World War.'

'That explains this, then,' said Luke, scratching around in the tin and bringing out a small pewter object. 'It's a badge!' He held it in his open hand. Above a number 12 stood a proud kangaroo. Beneath that were the letters ALH and written on a scroll were the words, VIRTUTIS FORTUNA COMES.

'Fortune favours the brave,' said Steve, looking over Luke's shoulder. 'The motto of the Twelfth Light Horse Regiment. They're legendary around these parts – table-lands boys, many of them were, on tablelands horses.'

He pointed up to the mountains. 'Remember I told you those brumbies you're so fond of are all direct descendants of the Walers, the horses that carried our boys into battle.'

'That's right,' said Jess.

'It's well documented,' said Steve. 'The station folk bred them for the remount trade during the war. They would run 'em wild in the bush, release good stallions, then muster them up and let the boys buck 'em out.' He laughed. 'Legend has it there were rodeos going on all over these mountains. The bush boys stuck to the saddles like glue and one after the other the horses were broken in and led away to the Light Horse training camps at Armidale.'

Jess read the date on the small box again. 'In October, same as the brumby massacre.'

'Yes,' said Steve in a grim voice. 'Eighty-three years later, almost to the day. Instead of celebrating those horses, they slaughtered their descendants. Bloody shameful, if you ask me.'

'Disgraceful,' agreed Jess. She imagined all those wild brumbies being run out of the bush, broken in, put on ships and taken to a foreign land where they were ridden into a storm of bullets.

'Not one of them came home,' said Steve. 'Too costly for the government. The soldiers had to shoot them.'

'So, these ones, the ones in the mountains now . . .'

'When the Twelfth Regiment disbanded, switched to vehicles, they released a lot of the cavalry horses back into the mountains. The wild horses around here are their descendants. Or they were, before the government decided to shoot them all.'

'So, who was Private Gordon Robertson and why are all his treasures stuffed in the wall of this house?' wondered Jess.

'That was my grandparents' name,' said Luke. 'My mother's maiden name.'

Everyone stared at Luke.

'It was,' he said. 'My grandfather's name was Frank Robertson. He was my mother's dad.'

'That's right,' said Steve. 'That was Matty's name, before she married Jack.'

Luke kept carefully unfolding the papers. They cracked and split at the creases as he spread them out, one by one on top of each other. Some were forms, typed with clunky bold font, filled out with fancy handwritten calligraphy and sealed with wax stamps. They had signatures scrawled on them with ink that seeped into the thick paper and left bleed marks.

Luke opened several papers that were folded together. 'Receipts,' he said. 'Made out to a Laura Robertson. Hey, looks like Granny Robertson was a horse dealer!'

He held one of the documents out in front of him. '"Paid to Laura Robertson, the sum of one hundred and ninety-two pounds, for the purchase of twelve Walers."' He flipped through the others. 'And here's one for twenty-three Walers, another one for six . . .'

'She'd have been selling them for the remount trade too,' said Steve. 'Told you! It was good money.'

'What else is there?'

'A birth certificate,' said Mrs Arnold, rummaging through a different pile of papers. 'Granny Robertson had a kid, Frank, born in 1932, so she must have been your *great*-grandmother.' She lifted the certificate and looked underneath it. 'And another one, an Elizabeth Jane. Oh, here's little Lizzie's death certificate. She died as an infant.'

'Why would all this be stuffed inside the wall of the house?' asked Luke.

'Maybe they hid their worldly goods and went on the road looking for work,' said Mrs Arnold. 'They were tough times back then. They were the Depression years.'

Luke unfolded more paper and squinted to read the faded print. He fingered the paper.

'New South Wales Department of Lands . . . *This Indenture made by the* . . . I can't read that bit . . . *on the* . . . must be the date . . . *Year of the Reign of our Sovereign, Defender of the Faith and in the year of our Lord God* . . . Geez, they go on with some waffle,' he said, casting the document aside and reaching for another.

Jess picked it up and scanned it. Most of it was so faded that she couldn't read it, and the language was obscure, but she could make out words like *towns*, *lands*, *tenements* and *hereby granted* . . . 'Is this some sort of thing about owning land?' she asked. 'It also says something about the Shire of New England . . . "Granted by the Crown in recognition of service . . ."'

'A land grant,' said Steve, peering over her shoulder. 'Twenty square miles, most of them were, none of them fenced, neither.'

Before anyone could answer, Mrs Arnold, who had been squinting carefully at another document, erupted. 'Certificate of marriage! Gordon Robertson and Laura Margaret *Mathews*,' she said, triumphantly. 'Holy horse dealers, old Granny Robertson's maiden name was *Mathews*! These documents belong to the original settlers.'

Everyone crowded around Mrs Arnold, grabbing at her and trying to get a better look at the piece of paper. She held it in the air. 'Righto, righto, no need to mug me!'

'Excuse me,' said an indignant Luke. 'I think I should get first look.'

The others backed off and Luke held his hand out to Mrs Arnold. She handed it to him. 'Gentle, it's a bit crumbly.'

Luke carefully opened it out in his palms. 'Gordon Robertson and Laura Margaret Mathews,' he said in a voice filled with wonder.

'Kwor,' Grace breathed. 'You know what that means . . .'

Jess's skin began to prickle. Luke looked stupefied.

Everyone's eyes danced as the possibility percolated through their imaginations. If they were right, Luke was a descendant of the Mathews family, the original settlers of this valley. The owners of Brumby Mountain. And since no one else had come forward to claim the land, Luke might be the last one left.

'I think we better get all that stuff to a solicitor,' said Lawson. He grinned and smacked Luke wholeheartedly on the back. 'Time to lodge a claim, bro!'

'Reckon?' said Luke.

'It's as much yours as anyone else's,' said Mrs Arnold. She threw her car keys to Lawson. 'Go now. Let's get this sorted, once and for all.'

28

WHILE LAWSON AND LUKE raced to Armidale with the new-found documents, Jess helped finish stacking the timber onto a pile, ready to burn. She worked with a mixture of feelings. She was excited for Luke and about all the hope that was coming for the brumbies on the mountain. But she didn't dare acknowledge what it might mean for her.

The afternoon dragged on into long hours of anxiety, sweat and decaying timber. The harder she worked, the more she could focus on her aching limbs instead of the possibility that she might lose Luke for good.

The sun was sinking behind the mountain by the time the fourbie rattled back along the dirt road and rolled in through the gate. Luke emerged from the car looking victorious.

Jess wiped her grimy hands on an old torn rag and walked slowly to the car. 'What did the solicitor say?'

'I only spoke to him quickly. I've got a real appointment on Monday. But he said it's worth a shot. He's going to go through all the papers and if they're good I can lodge the claim.' Luke grabbed Jess in a huge bear hug and swung her around. 'It'll be a brumby sanctuary, Jessy!'

She squeezed him back. 'Just like that?'

'Well . . .' Luke caught his breath suddenly and put her back down, as though common sense had caught up with him. 'We won't know for ages. These things take years, decades even. But the claim is lodged – well, it will be on Monday. We have enough material to interrupt the sale of the place. They can't auction it off while we keep the process going.'

'Let's release the mares,' said Grace, bouncing up behind them.

'Yeah!' said Shara.

And as though it had heard them talking, a horse called from the outer rims of the property. It was a long, enquiring whinny.

'Did you hear that?' laughed Grace. 'They want us to hurry up!'

'Let's do it before it gets dark,' said Jess.

'Brumbies can probably see in the dark anyway,' said Grace. 'These girls would know the mountains like the backs of their hooves!'

They all walked to the river. Lawson swung himself

into the driver's seat and drove the truck closer to the river crossing.

'Hey, you've branded them,' said Jess, as the mares came out quietly, clomping down the tailgate one cautious hoof at a time. On each horse's shoulder was a fresh scab: a capital M inside a larger capital C. 'Whose brand is that?'

'Mine,' said Luke, smiling. 'MC, for Matty's Creek. Lawson helped me make it. I'm going to register it, too.'

There was no pause at the bottom of the ramp, only acceleration, and Jess felt her anxiety ease, replaced by warm satisfaction at the sight of the horses' pricked ears and instantly brighter eyes. The lead mare, the bay, walked to the river crossing, lifted her nose and whinnied. The second mare, the creamy one, nickered, and from the densely treed hills came answering cries.

'I can't believe how much calmer they are now that they're home,' Jess said. 'It's as if they just know all their troubles are over.' She noticed an amused smile lurking beneath Lawson's deadpan face. 'What?'

He snorted and looked away.

'What?' she demanded again.

Lawson smirked. 'One of the reasons they're calmer is that Biyanga gave them a quick going-away present before they left Coachwood Crossing.'

Jess gasped. How could she not have noticed? Luke's jaw also dropped.

'I had to bring them into the yards to brand them anyway.' Lawson gave one of his uproarious laughs and slapped Luke on the back. 'Think of it as a housewarming pressie. We'll come back in a few years and do some trapping.'

The mares broke into a canter, and splashed through the river with their tails high.

By the time Lawson had stopped laughing, the brumbies were gone. The whinnying stopped and Jess imagined the reassuring nuzzling and nickering that would be going on in the gully beyond. She imagined the tiny seeds the mares carried inside them; the genes of the great campdraft sire, Biyanga. What better blood to replace the lost stallions and to mix with the spirits of Saladin? There would be some awesome horses roaming the mountain in future years.

'Are you ready to light this up, Luke?' Lawson called over his shoulder as he walked towards the pile. 'It's your place. You do the honours!' He tossed over a box of matches.

'You bet.' Luke snatched them out of the air and walked to the enormous stack of timber. 'This place could do with a good smoking. Get all the ghosts out of here.'

'I reckon,' agreed Jess.

Luke struck a match and dropped it on the kero-soaked timber at the bottom of the stack. It ignited with an air-sucking *woof*, and quickly lapped up through the beams and rails and half-rotten fenceposts, sheets of plywood and sacks of rubbish. Within minutes it was burning brightly, with twisting flames reaching upwards and sending glowing sparks whirling high into the night.

'Now that's what I call a housewarming,' said Lawson.

'Yep,' said Luke, stepping back and holding an arm up to shield his face from the intense glare. 'That there is a warm house.'

As the flames fed on the rubble, things fizzed and popped and snapped. Pieces collapsed, and tiny grey flakes wafted around in the glowing orange light. Thick black smoke billowed into the dimming sky.

'That is filthy dirty smoke,' noted Jess.

'It is,' said Luke. 'It'll get cleaner as all the paint and rubbish goes and it gets back to plain wood.'

'Wood that was probably cut from these hillsides.'

Luke nodded. 'Ashes to ashes.'

Corey and Tom were already rolling out their swags, and Filth and Fang bounded all over them, much to the boys' annoyance. They yelled at the big dirty dogs to get off. Mrs Arnold was in her favourite fold-out chair with a glass of port in hand and Lawson sat on a log nearby, looking up at the flames. He reached behind him and pulled a banjo onto his lap.

Jess took her swag from the truck, rolled it out under

a tree and lay on her belly with her chin in her hands. Above the crackle of the fire she could hear the frogs in the river. Luke, she noticed, set up his swag next to Tom and Corey.

Luke was strangely remote from her all night. He was polite, too formal, his conversation was awkward and she could tell he was intentionally hanging with the boys, keeping the chiacking going on longer than was comfortable for anyone. She watched the way he moved, with quick, sharp motions, always underlined with nervous energy.

As Jess lay on her swag, watching the flames dissolve his past into his future, she felt the pieces click together with a sudden, painful snap.

Tomorrow, this river-flat property would be cleansed of the bruised and troubled brumby spirits – and the heartbroken human ones, too. Tomorrow, she would leave this beautiful place and go back to Coachwood Crossing.

Tonight, though, there was nothing but the sounds of buzzing insects, a crackling fire and a possum searching for fruits in the fig tree overhead. There was the banjo playing and Grace and Rosie singing ridiculous improvised versions of corny love songs. She would enjoy the here and now.

29

JESS WOKE, some time deep in the night, with Luke's hand brushing the hair off her face. She could feel the breath from his nose, cool and soft on her skin. She shifted her chin and kissed him without bothering to open her eyes.

'Let's go for a night ride,' she heard him say softly.

She opened her eyes and found his, only centimetres away. But his smile was somehow forced. He didn't kiss her.

'Sure,' she said, trying to keep her voice even. She pushed her blanket off, pulled on her jeans and a jumper and followed him to the river crossing, where Rambo nibbled at the grass along its edges. He raised his head and nickered.

Luke put an arm around the old horse's neck and held out a hand to leg Jess up. She eased herself on and felt Luke leap up behind her. As they rode into the mountain, she felt as though she was riding to a funeral and she steeled herself for the news that was to come.

Rambo took them deep into the mountain, up across hillsides and down into gorges so rugged and dark that Jess could barely see her hand in front of her. They rode surrounded by wispy shapes in shades and layers and mysterious patches of blackness until the mountain became completely black. All Jess could feel was the swaying motion of the horse beneath her and Luke's body, swinging in time. The terrain was so rugged that at times she couldn't tell if they were travelling uphill or downhill. She could hear squeaks and wind and rustling all around her, Rambo's hooves brushing through grasses, and Luke breathing.

The whole time they were riding, Luke didn't speak. And the further they travelled, the worse Jess imagined the news would be.

'Where is he taking us?' Jess finally whispered. She grabbed hold of a chunk of mane as she felt Rambo's shoulders drop down beneath her.

'I don't know,' Luke answered, as they rose again and Rambo's hooves scrambled in front of Jess.

'I'm cold.'

Luke unzipped his jacket and wrapped it around her. She felt his chin rest on her shoulder. His hair warmed the side of her face.

They rode aimlessly through the trees and the shrubs for the entire night, and if it wasn't for the fact that she felt it would be her last ride with Luke, Jess would have turned back hours earlier. But she didn't want it to end. Every moment that was offered to her in this achingly beautiful place, with him, she would take. They rode through bitter cold and she felt the contrast between the sharp ice of her feet and the warmth of Luke's body wrapped around hers.

Through the gullies around her, Jess could hear water gurgling, thousands of tiny trickles, running down tree trunks and dripping from strings of bark, seeping between rocks, cutting little pathways to the creek. And as they rode, the sound grew louder, larger, until it culminated in a waterfall, gushing and plunging over granite cliffs.

Rambo plodded steadily downhill and walked straight into the falls. Suddenly, dramatically, the sounds changed to long, hollow echoes. The air was cool and moist and smelled of horses. Jess realised they were riding through a dark tunnel inside the mountain. Water seeped through the rocks and plipped into puddles beneath. Rambo's steady clopping over the moist earth floor sounded like a slow drumbeats. Luke's arms tightened around her.

When Jess could hardly bear the creepiness of it any longer, she saw light, a tiny glow, steadily increasing.

Daybreak. The light grew steadily as they rode closer; a corridor of greys and soft pre-dawn blues before them.

They emerged onto a rock platform and Jess caught her breath at the scene before her. Mist and cloud hovered around and over the mountains. Below, as though at the bottom of a deep, wide well, were horses, dozens of them, grazing alongside each other. Surrounding them in all directions were perfectly vertical cliffs, immense granite columns. At first glance, it seemed there was no way in and no way out.

The horses were spread over the wide grassy hollow, a mix of creamy colours: buckskins, palominos, chestnuts and a few bays. Some were shorter, some taller, but they were all cut from the same stuff. Jess spotted Stormy-girl, the old coloured mare, and her stallion grazing together on the edge of the mob. There was more than one creamy colt and many younger foals.

They sat silently watching the smoke from a distant fire seep in with the early-morning fog. And as the sun rose, big and fiery and beautiful, it vaporised the clouds. A great golden eagle soaring on the wings of the wind hovered overhead, and Jess imagined Sapphire's spirit free again, inextinguishable, being carried back to his home and his family.

'Sapphire's home,' she muttered to herself. Then she turned to Luke. 'You're both home.'

'It's not my home,' he said quietly. 'It's theirs.' He looked out over the brumbies, and his eyes were sharp and bright. 'I'd never live here.'

'Really?'

'Everything's too cold,' he said, and this time his voice had laughter on the edges of it. 'The rivers are freezing. And I have to put my shoes on all the time.'

'That would suck.'

Luke grinned down at her, his wild bushy hair whipping around his face. 'This place will wait, Jessy. My place is with you.'

It came to her, in a sudden start, that he was coming home. There was a bond between him and this mountain. But she realised now he could leave it and still carry it with him, this small piece of the world with its gullies and ridges and trundling wombats, its tall messy ribbon gums and grasses that waved and floated in the icy mountain winds. The birds that twittered in the swampy heath and the roos that bounded over the fences. And the creamy blue-eyed brumbies that ran with Saladin's spirit (and Biyanga's now, too!), and the locals that gathered around the pub fire at night, sharing stories and warm schooners of port.

The place gave Luke an identity and at any time he could look inside himself and reaffirm who he was, find the mountains and the rivers and the wild horses that drank from its edges. He was the son of Matilda and Jack and a son of Mathews' Flat.

But he had already been there a lifetime, she realised. If not in body, then in spirit. His life, his story, was etched into the place. He didn't need to live here to know he belonged.

Jess cast her eyes across the mountain and let herself drift for a moment in its never-ending beauty. Then, dawdling a little, she gathered a lump of Rambo's mane and legged him back down the brumby trail.

Acknowledgements

SPECIAL THANKS to my beautiful girls, Annabelle and Ruby, for being so good and patient while Mum's been locked away working, to Anthony for your endless love and support, and to my mum for looking after my little wildies so I could write.

Thanks to Katherine Waddington of the Australian Brumby Alliance for your encouragement, stories, photos, experiences and knowledge about wild horses; to Kath Massey of the Hunter Valley Brumby Association, and to Christine O'Rourke from Guy Fawkes Heritage Horse Association for showing me your beautiful Guy Fawkes horses.

Not nearly enough credit is given to editors, designers, marketing teams and publishing pros in the success of a book. It takes so many more people than just a lone author. So, to the entire team at Allen & Unwin, whose skills and talent have made my books come to life, my heartfelt thanks. And another extra-special thanks to my publisher, Sarah Brenan, and my editor, Hilary Reynolds; I learn so much more every time I work with you.

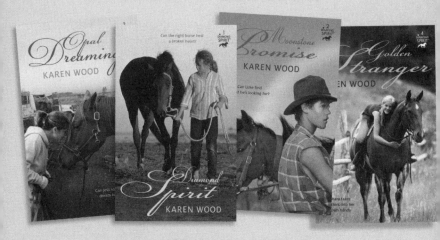

Have you read the first four books in the Diamond Spirit series?

'The best books I have ever read – I love all the drama and romance.' RENEE

'Thank you thank you thank you for writing my all-time favourite book series ever!' ELISE

'I just get completely lost in your books – I really feel like I am there.' MEG

About the Author

KAREN WOOD has been involved with horses for most of her life. Her most special horse is a little chestnut stockhorse called Reo (who does share some common ancestry with Saladin, via Radium). Karen is married with two children and lives on the Central Coast, New South Wales.

www.diamondspirit.net